A Haunted Mine Is a
Terrible Thing to Waste

Look for these SpineChillers™ Mysteries

SpineChillers™
Mysteries

A Haunted Mine Is a Terrible Thing to Waste

Fred E. Katz

Tommy
NELSON™

Thomas Nelson, Inc.
Nashville

Published in Nashville, Tennessee, by Tommy Nelson™, a division of Thomas Nelson, Inc. SpineChillers™ Mysteries is a trademark of Thomas Nelson, Inc.

Library of Congress Cataloging-in-Publication Data

Katz, Fred E.
    A Haunted mine is a terrible thing to waste / Fred E. Katz.
        p.   cm. — (SpineChillers™ mysteries ; 12)
    Summary: When twelve-year-old Boone and his church group set up a camp on the site of an abandoned mining town, they need to resolve weird happenings on the premises.
    ISBN 0-8499-4055-9
    [1. Horror stories. 2. Christian life—Fiction. 3. Camps—Fiction.] I. Title.
II. Series: Katz, Fred E.   SpineChillers™ mysteries ; 12.
PZ7.K1573Hau   1997
[Fic]—dc21

                                                                97-35639
                                                                     CIP
                                                                      AC

Printed in the United States of America

98 99 00 01 02 QKP 9 8 7 6 5 4 3 2 1

"Wow!" I shouted as I twisted in my seat to take in the peaks that surrounded us. I couldn't believe the awesome mountains we could see from this high valley. As I stared out the pickup truck window, we entered camp. The remains of a dozen or so old buildings greeted us. "Is this Camp Fearless?" I asked, surprised.

"Yep, Boone, it sure is. Looks like it needs a little work, doesn't it?" As he spoke, Mr. Ramos, my neighbor and friend from church, turned the steering wheel to avoid another pothole in the dirt road.

"I'd say it needs a *lot* of work. This place looks pretty beat up to me," I said.

"I guess if you didn't have any tender loving care for nearly fifty years, you'd look a little run down too," Mr. Ramos said as we stopped in front of one of the buildings. I couldn't read the weathered paint on the sign over its door. But the structure looked like it must have been the general store.

"Mr. Ramos, why hasn't anyone lived in this town for so long?" I asked.

"No one's lived here since the old mine ran dry. And right now, I'm really glad the town was abandoned," he answered.

"Why is that?" I asked.

"Remember Mr. Markham from church? He's owned the town of Fearless for years, but he's never done any repair work here. If he had, he might have sold it instead of donating it to the church. That's just one of the wonderful ways that God provides for his people."

"And if he hadn't donated the land, we'd still be looking for a place to hold our church camp," I added.

"Right," Mr. Ramos agreed. "Let's get out and have a look. I guess we're the first to get here."

I climbed out of the pickup and wandered around. "Doesn't look much like the church camp I went to last summer," I remarked as I walked back toward Mr. Ramos.

"I guess not, but with some hard work, we can make this place great," he encouraged.

I didn't answer. I had a hard time believing Camp Fearless would ever look good. I walked away again to study several old cabins. Their shingles were gray with age. Some of them looked like they needed new roofs. My grandmother had always told me to look for the potential in things. I tried hard, but I wondered whether Fearless could ever become a good place for campers.

"A coat of paint will do wonders," Mr. Ramos called cheerfully, jarring me out of my thoughts.

"Yeah, maybe. How many people are coming to help?" I asked.

"We have seven men and women from the church. And Cali Bittner is coming with her parents," he answered.

I counted.

"Ten total," I gasped. I didn't finish my thought out loud. *Ten people to fix this dump up. . . . A hundred people might do the trick.* With only eight adults and two middle schoolers, we had a huge task ahead of us. I found it hard to believe that we'd even scratch the surface this weekend.

I had to admit that having Cali along would make the job a lot more fun. When our Sunday school class collected food for the needy last Thanksgiving, we'd been partners. We'd collected more than any other team. And we'd had a great time working together.

I stepped onto the front porch of one of the cabins to look inside. My weight made the floorboards creak. For a moment I thought it sounded like a wild animal's cry. A chill worked its way up my spine.

"That mountain wind can be chilly," Mr. Ramos said. "You'd better grab your jacket. Believe me, it'll only get colder as the day goes on."

3

"A jacket sounds like a good idea. I just felt a little chill," I answered. I decided to blame my shiver on the cold. But as I walked to the truck, something made me look back over my shoulder. For just a second, I was certain someone was watching me. It was as if there were eyes somewhere in the woods peering right at me.

I tried to shake off the feeling as I put on my old denim jacket. I looked up at the sky. The sun was out. The sky was blue. Why had I suddenly felt a chill?

Mr. Ramos watched me check out the sky and smiled. "Come look at this," he called to me across the camp.

I jogged over to where he stood.

"Know what this is?" he asked.

I studied the round stone wheel. I shook my head. "I don't think so," I admitted. "Can you tell me?"

"It's an old grindstone," he said.

"Is that what I'm supposed to keep my nose to?" I joked.

"Nose to the grindstone. That's pretty funny, Boone," Mr. Ramos said with a wink. "This grindstone was probably used to sharpen tools like shovels and hoes."

"And axes," said a low, mysterious voice behind me

4

I jumped and turned toward the voice. Even Mr. Ramos seemed to snap to attention.

"Sorry, I didn't mean ta frighten ya." An older man with white hair stood behind us. I wondered how he had gotten there without our hearing him. His body looked thin and hunched over, and he hadn't shaved for several days. When he smiled, I saw that he was missing a front tooth.

"Ezra Pike's the name," the man said as he offered his hand to Mr. Ramos. "I sorta keep my eye on the old place. Kinda like a caretaker, I reckon."

"Nice to meet you. We didn't expect to find anyone up here. I'm Luis Ramos, and this is my young neighbor Boone Colby."

"Y'all here as part of the church-goin' folks that are plannin' on fixin' this place up?" he asked.

"Yes, sir," Mr. Ramos said with a smile. "And it looks as if we've got our work cut out for us."

"I guess I best be wishin' ya luck," the mysterious Mr. Pike said.

"Several others will be joining us for the weekend."

"That'll help some. You folks'll still be plenty busy. Joshua Markham told me that you planned on openin' up this here church camp by July," the old man remarked.

"God willing, that is our target date," Mr. Ramos agreed.

Ezra Pike shook his white hair and rubbed a rough hand over the stubble on his chin. "I 'spect ya won't be seein' that dream come true. Not unless ya got a right big group of people comin' ta help. These old cabins need lotsa work."

"Oh, but we're not going to use the cabins. At least, not at first. This weekend we're going to focus on just one or two buildings—to be used as a dining and meeting hall. Our campers will sleep in tents until we have the time and money to rebuild the cabins. I expect that to take several years," Mr. Ramos told the older man.

"Don't know as I'd wanna sleep in a tent up here," the caretaker said. His gaze took in the town, then he looked right at me. "Not with what I know about this ol' ghost town."

"Ghost town?" I blurted out. I felt my mouth go dry.

"Don't get too excited, Boone. A ghost town is just

6

a town that nobody lives in any longer," Mr. Ramos said quickly. "This used to be a bustling mining town. When the mine dried up, the people moved out. But that doesn't mean there are ghosts here."

The caretaker gave a little laugh. "I didn't say there were any ghosts." He hesitated a moment as if thinking, then added, "At least none that I've actually seen." The old man placed his hand on my shoulder and asked, "How old are ya then, young man?"

"Twelve, sir," I answered.

"Well," the man said with surprise, "twelve, ya say? You're right tall for a twelve-year-old, aren't ya?"

"Yeah, I guess so." I was glad the subject had moved off ghosts, or whatever the caretaker thought he'd seen in Fearless.

Without warning, the old man turned on his heel and began to walk away. "I'll leave ya to yer hard work. If y'all need anything, give a holler. I live in the cabin yonder, across the dry creek bed," he said as he left us.

Mr. Ramos and I looked at each other, confused by this man's sudden actions.

Ezra Pike had walked about a hundred yards away when he abruptly turned and headed back again. "Nearly forgot to tell ya what I come ta tell ya. The water in the well is sweet and good ta drink, but ya gotta git it by pumpin' that handle," he said as he indicated the pump. "That'll be a good chore for the boy. Oh, and one other thing." He stopped for a moment and took a deep breath. "The land belonging to Fearless runs up this valley. Right to the top of that ridge." He pointed as he spoke.

I turned to look at the beautiful mountain ridge that bordered Camp Fearless.

Mr. Pike continued, "You church folk can hike anywhere this side of that there ridge. It belongs to you now. Just don't cross over it. That land beyond is the Atlas Ski Resort's. And they don't cotton ta folks traipsing on their property."

"I'll tell the others," Mr. Ramos promised.

"Good. Well, I'll be a gettin' along," the caretaker said. He pulled a large red handkerchief from his back pocket. Shaking it with a snap, he wiped his brow as he strolled away.

We watched as Mr. Pike crossed the dry creek bed. Once he was out of sight, Mr. Ramos suggested that we explore what would become Camp Fearless. While my friend looked for the best building to convert to a dining hall, I wandered around the ghost town, wishing the caretaker hadn't used that phrase.

I kept one eye on the woods around us and the other on the windows of the various buildings. There was something about Fearless I didn't like. Something felt wrong in this old mining town. I knew there was a mystery here to solve. I couldn't wait for Cali to arrive to help me.

While I thought about everything I wanted to tell Cali, I wandered aimlessly around Fearless.

Suddenly, something grabbed my ankle and I crashed to the ground.

The next thing I knew I felt fingers wrapping themselves around my arm. In my momentary panic, I wondered if ghosts had fingers.

"Are you okay?" I heard Mr. Ramos ask from above me. Then I realized it was his hand around my arm. He helped me to my feet as he said, "It looks like we'd better be careful in all these weeds. This old piece of a horse's harness was lurking and waiting for someone just like you to come along and fall over it."

I could only grin sheepishly. "I guess I need to keep my eyes on where I'm going. I got kind of distracted looking at all these old buildings. It's like something out of a cowboy movie—only for real."

I let my gaze travel up the steep hillside behind

the general store. Something moved between two large pine trees. I caught my breath. Was it just the wind blowing the underbrush?

But I was pretty sure I had seen something. And it didn't look . . . well, human. Or like any animal I knew. What was it?

I shaded my eyes to get a better look. Nothing moved up there now. Maybe it had been just a shadow. Yeah, that had to be it. I'd seen a shadow.

"I think we should set up our tents in this meadow. What do you think, Boone?" Mr. Ramos's voice startled me. I'd almost forgotten he was standing beside me.

I stammered out, "It's a nice spot, I guess." Suddenly I shivered again. What was wrong with me? It wasn't that cold out here. I absently followed my older friend as he examined some of the buildings.

"I'll bet that was the blacksmith's shop," Mr. Ramos said, pointing toward a building. "And that was the village church, between those two cabins. See the steeple? That should be our second project. I think it would be great to hold services in it."

We walked toward the old church. I hadn't taken more than three steps when I heard a low moaning. It grew louder. The sound seemed to come from the right. I started. "What's that?"

"Just the wind in the trees," Mr. Ramos said peacefully. "Listen to it. That's nature's music." He threw back his head and gazed at the blue sky. "Isn't this the most beautiful place you've ever seen?"

He turned his attention back to the church. Trying to shake my foolish fear, I asked, "I wonder how many people once worshiped in this little church?"

Mr. Ramos shook his head. "It doesn't look very big, but I bet lots of folks have come here over the years. I pray that our whole church will be able to worship up here as well." We began to climb the stairs as he spoke.

"Be careful," Mr. Ramos warned. "These wood steps may be a little rotten."

I stamped my foot. The boards seemed solid.

When we tried the door we found it unlocked. A hinge squeaked as the door swung back. Together we walked down the aisle toward the altar.

"Well, it's clear that no one has worshiped here in a long time. This place needs a good cleaning. But except for the cobwebs, it seems in good shape. Maybe this doesn't have to be a big project. I don't see why we can't hold the camp's services in here."

Vehicles pulling up outside interrupted our discussion.

"It sounds like everyone else is here," I said.

I hurried to the door and looked outside. I watched as a car, a van, and another pickup truck pulled in behind Mr. Ramos's truck.

For some reason I felt better now that we weren't alone. Like my grandmother used to tell me, there's safety in numbers.

As we hurried out to meet the others, Mr. Ramos pulled the church door shut behind him.

I shot a quick glance toward the hill behind the general store. Nothing looked unusual. Yet I knew I had seen something up there. Had it just been an animal? Or had someone—or something—been up there watching us? Cali waved when she spotted me.

"Hi, Cali," I called. I was glad I had someone my own age to talk with. Maybe she could help me solve the mystery of Camp Fearless. I bet she could find a logical reason for the creepy feeling I had.

Mr. Ramos took the next several minutes to get everyone organized.

Cali and I helped her parents set up a place to have our meals. Mr. Ramos sent three people to check out the buildings he thought were the safest. Together they would decide which to begin working on. The others helped Mr. Ramos unload the vehicles.

"Why don't you and Cali set up these tents in that little meadow?" Mr. Ramos suggested after we'd cleared a cooking area. My friend had his hands full of tents and pegs.

"Sure thing," I answered as a I gave Cali a quick inquiring look. "Have you ever set up a tent before?"

"No problem, Boone. My family is the original Swiss Family Robinson. We go camping all the time," she answered with her biggest grin.

We carried the bags of tents over to the meadow. Cali patiently explained how to set them up. In no time, I got the hang of what I needed to do.

"We camped in a place like this last summer," Cali said as she drove a tent peg into the ground.

She dumped the second tent out of its bag.

"Here. Help me spread this out flat," she requested.

As we worked, Cali glanced back toward the buildings. She squinted her blue eyes against the sunlight, and ran a hand through her long, blond hair. I watched as she chewed on her lower lip.

"Something wrong?" I asked.

Cali shook her head and tried to return her attention to the tent. But I noticed she kept looking over her shoulder.

"Cali, what's the matter?" I asked.

"Nothing. Really." Cali reached for a tent pole. But she seemed preoccupied.

I had an idea what was bothering her. I tried to get her to tell me by joking with her.

"I know. You're afraid that the others will eat all the food while we slave away out here," I quipped.

Cali laughed. Then she said, "I don't know. Maybe it's just all these old deserted buildings. But something's kind of giving me the creeps."

"I know what you mean. When I first got here, I thought that something was . . ."

"Watching us," she blurted out.

I looked up and my eyes met hers. She whispered hopefully, "An animal?"

"Or a ghost. An old caretaker stopped by earlier and called this place a ghost town."

"This place is suddenly giving me the spooks," Cali said with a shiver. "A few minutes ago I thought I saw some kind of movement near the trees. But everyone else is by the trucks and the buildings."

"I've had that same spooky feeling since we got here." I was glad to share my fears.

"You have?"

"I thought I saw something move up on the side of the hill earlier. Above the general store. It didn't look like an animal. If it was a person, why didn't it step out of the shadows?" I asked.

Cali chewed on her lower lip again. "Maybe someone doesn't want us to know we're being watched. Maybe we're being spied on." She hesitated.

A scream shattered the silence between us. It came from the direction of the old general store.

"Help me! Help!"

"That's my mother!" Cali yelled in alarm as she sprinted toward the old building.

"Help!" Mrs. Bittner cried out again. "I'm stuck!"

I dashed after Cali. My heart pounded. I had known something terrible was going to happen.

"Mom!" Cali screamed as she dashed toward the general store.

I caught up to her at the store's wide front porch.

"Don't come in. Stay out there," her mother called to us through the open door.

"Mom, what's wrong? What happened?"

I peered over Cali's shoulder. For a few seconds I couldn't see anything in the gloomy interior. My eyes had to adjust after being out in the bright sun.

"I came in to check out the old store," Mrs. Bittner explained. "Without warning, a piece of the floor gave way beneath my feet. I managed to stop the fall with my arms, but I'm dangling between the boards. My feet aren't touching anything, and I'm not sure how much longer I can hold myself up."

Cali had carefully edged into the room. When I saw Mrs. Bittner, I felt my knees go weak with relief. She didn't seem hurt. But she certainly needed help.

"Be careful, Cali," her mom urged as Cali started slowly toward her.

"I will."

"I'll get a rope," I volunteered. Then I raced out to the truck.

Cali worked her way to her mother, stopping every few steps to test the floor.

"It seems solid," she said. "Why do you suppose just one part of the floor is rotten? That doesn't make sense."

I raced back to the doorway with the rope in my hand. "Cali, I'll toss one end of the rope to you. Tie it tightly around your waist. If the floor gives way under you, you won't fall through into the basement."

Cali caught the end of the rope and tied it carefully around her waist.

I secured the other end around the porch banister.

"Ready," I said. "Be careful."

Cali nodded. She got down on her hands and knees and crawled forward. The floor didn't even creak.

"A piece of floorboard has snagged the back of my sweatshirt," Mrs. Bittner said. "If you can get it loose, I think you can pull me out of here."

Cali moved around her mother and saw the jagged end of the board. She reached for it. To her surprise, when she pulled upward, it broke off easily.

"What a relief," Mrs. Bittner said with a sigh.

"Cali, do you think the floor will hold me too?" I asked.

"I think so," Cali replied, "but watch your step; this board just snapped off in my hands."

"Maybe just that one section is bad. I'm coming to help," I told her.

Moments later Cali and I pulled her mom to safety. As we did, we broke another floorboard. But when I pulled on the next board, it wouldn't budge. How strange.

Cali's mom thanked us for rescuing her, then she added, "Well, I always did like to jump feet first into a new project."

Cali rolled her eyes at the bad joke. "If my mom's joking around then she's not hurt," she said to me.

"I think I'm done exploring for a while," Mrs. Bittner told us with a grin. "And it's getting close to noon. Maybe we should grab the others and have some lunch."

Mrs. Bittner headed out to round up the adults. Cali and I stopped for a moment to untie the rope from her waist. When her mom was out of earshot, Cali leaned toward me and whispered, "I want to take a better look at those floorboards later on."

"Why?" I asked.

"There's something odd about how they broke. Something's going on here, and I'm going to find out what. Boy, do I love—"

"A mystery," we said at the same time. Cali flashed me a smile.

"So what do you think happened here?" I asked.

"That floor is old but those boards didn't crumble like they were rotten. They snapped off clean. That's why I want to take another look at them."

We traded looks.

Cali nodded, "I don't feel good about this place."

"That makes two of us," I told her. I looked around slowly.

"Come on, kids. Let's eat," someone called to us.

Until I saw the food, I hadn't realized how hungry I was. I ate quickly and went back for seconds.

While I was standing near the food, Cali finished eating, got up, and started toward the trash bag with her plate. Something made her glance up at the sky.

"Oh no!" she screamed. Then she dropped her paper plate. In one quick motion, she ducked her head and covered her face with her hands.

I spun around at the sound. Cali was cowering near the ground.

Then I saw what had frightened her. A huge black bird was swooping toward her from the top of a nearby pine tree. With its wings close to its body, it hurtled down surprisingly fast.

The bird opened its yellow beak and gave a harsh cry. When it was only a foot or so from Cali, it spread its wings and stretched out its claws.

As we watched, the bird's feet closed around a piece of bread that had been on Cali's plate. Instantly the bird began to flap its wings hard. Within a few seconds, it had flown away to a grassy spot. It landed and began to peck at the crust of bread.

Cali looked at me and laughed nervously. "Why don't we go set up the rest of the tents? I think I want to do something a little less dangerous."

"Sure thing," I said. Together we went to the pickup to gather the rest of the tents.

Now that I'd had a little instruction, setting up the tents was an easy task. Within fifteen minutes we had them all set up.

"There," Cali said as she drove in the final tent peg. "Now everyone has a place to sleep."

"Should we go join the adults?" I asked. "It sounds like everyone is hard at work."

"First I want to go back to the general store. I want to take a good look at those floorboards."

"Do you really think it's safe? I don't want to end up in the basement the hard way."

Cali shrugged and started toward the old general store. I decided to follow her. Maybe I could at least keep her out of trouble.

"I'm not too worried about falling through the floor," she said slowly. "Everywhere we walked seemed solid enough."

"Then why did your mother break through?" I wondered aloud.

"That's exactly what we need to find out."

Moments later we peered through the open door.

"It's sure spooky and full of shadows in here," Cali said. Her voice was just above a whisper.

"It does seem kind of creepy," I agreed. "In fact, everything about this place has been kind of creepy."

"Yeah, even lunch," Cali remarked. She drew in a breath. "Let's wait a minute to give our eyes time to adjust. Then it won't be so hard to see."

While we were waiting, I heard a noise inside the building. "What's that?" I asked as I tried to make out what had made the sound. "It sounded like it came from there." I pointed. "Back where it's darkest."

Cali and I peered into the dim corner. We both saw something move at about the same time.

"A mouse," she whispered in relief.

Cali wandered cautiously inside. "Deep," she uttered.

"What?"

"The hole my mother fell into. Look how far she could have fallen. She's lucky she didn't get hurt badly," Cali said.

I peered into the hole. "Wow, it is deep. I'm glad God was watching out for your mom."

Cali moved away from the hole. Then she stamped her foot near the edge of one of the broken boards. It sounded solid.

"Cali, that board is still strong. In fact, none of the floorboards sound or look like they're rotten." I looked up at the ceiling and continued. "And the roof is still good; no rain could get though to rot them."

Cali reached down and picked up the wood she had broken away to free her mother.

"Hey, look at this!" she exclaimed.

"What?" I asked.

"Look at the edge of this board." She pointed at a deep groove in the wood. "See how bright and clean the wood is around that groove? I've been around my

21

dad's workshop enough to know this is a fresh cut."

I got down on my hands and knees and tried to peer under the edge of the flooring around the hole. I couldn't see anything, so I explored the underside of several boards with my hand.

"It feels like two grooves have been cut on the underside of this board," I said grimly.

"Does that mean what I think it does?" Cali asked.

I straightened up and moved back from the edge of the hole. "It means that someone deliberately scored those boards," I answered.

Cali nodded. "That's exactly what I thought. But why would anyone do that?"

"Someone wanted one of us to fall through."

Cali knelt down and felt beneath a board on the other side of the hole.

After a few seconds she said quietly, "Whoever did this made sure the hole would be fairly small. Those grooves are pretty close to each other."

"Oh, I get it. No one was supposed to fall all the way to the basement. It's like a warning. Your mom was able to stop herself and call for help."

"So, what do we do?" Cali asked.

"We keep our eyes and ears open," I said quickly. Then I added, "Let's find something to prove whether this little ghost town really has a ghost."

Cali shivered and said, "This is the spookiest place I've ever been in my life."

Before I could answer, we heard a creaking sound.

Suddenly a band of bright sunlight appeared across the floor. Someone, or something, was opening the store's side door. The sunlight stretched out like a finger, reaching toward us.

Into the band of light stepped a huge, grotesque figure. Its silhouette had two legs. But it also had a huge hump in the middle of its back, which almost reached above its head. I had no idea what sort of creature we were looking at.

"Boone!"

I heard the fear in Cali's whisper, but I was too frightened to answer her.

"Boone, it's heading right for us! What is it? What do we do?" she said in panic.

I stared at the open door. The thing with the huge hump filled the opening. Its shadow moved along the strip of brightness on the floor. When it moved, a beam of light struck its face.

"Mr. Pike!" I exclaimed and let out a breath. "What are you doing here?"

"What am I doin' here?" The caretaker growled. He scratched his beard stubble with his free hand. "I'm a-doin' my job. A better question'd be what're you doin' lurkin' in the darkness?" He dropped a huge plastic trash bag from his shoulder. Instead of waiting for me to answer, he continued, "I'm cleanin' up the trash left here by some past campers. Y'all come up here and throw yer garbage down and then head back to yer comfy homes, and I'm a stuck cleanin' up after ya."

Mr. Pike seemed to notice Cali for the first time. He forced his face into a grimace that passed for a smile. "Sorry 'bout that. I guess I was doin' a little preachin' there." He pulled his lips back farther. His missing tooth was more obvious than before. I watched as Cali squinted to get a better look at his face.

"No one from our church group will do that, sir. I assure you that we'll pick up all our trash before we leave," Cali said.

"That would be right nice. My word, little lady, where are my manners? I met your friend there earlier today. My name is Ezra Pike. I'm the care-taker 'round this place."

Mr. Pike reached up and scratched at his chin again. "I heard some of the others talkin' 'bout one of your womenfolk breakin' through the floor in this here buildin'."

"That was my mother," Cali volunteered.

"Well, the good Lord was clearly watchin' over her. Usually, when the Madman of the Mine sets out to git someone, he does."

"Madman of the Mine? What are you talking about?" I felt my heart begin to race again.

"Some'll say that he's a phantom, a product of over-active imaginations. I guess nobody wanted to scare you young'ns, but I'd watch my step if'n I was you," Mr. Pike said.

I felt a chill travel down my spine.

"What can you tell us about the Madman of the Mine, Mr. Pike?" Cali asked.

"Exactly where the legend came from has always been a mystery. I'm kinda partial ta the tale 'bout the man that lit a piece of dynamite. He throwed it inta the mine 'cos he'd thought he'd found a new vein o' silver and he didn' wanta share. He decided he'd kill his partner off and call it an accident. But the plan kinda backfired on him. Seems that ev'ryone 'ceptin' him got outa the mine alive. His spirit still roams through the mines guarding his silver," Mr. Pike said. "But the silver really played out years ago."

"Why would he come after my mother?" Cali asked. "She certainly wasn't after any silver."

"It don' matter. The Madman haunts this here mine. Rumor has it the people of Fearless cleared out when he started underminin' the town. Seems he liked ta weaken the wood in the buildings and

25

tunnels." The old caretaker looked from me to Cali and back to me again.

"Weaken the wood?" I asked.

"The Madman of the Mine'd cut gashes in the wood to weaken it. When the miners set off a dynamite blasts ta expose the silver ore, the weakened wood would give way. Several tunnels caved in and trapped the miners. Scared the resta them away."

"How did he cut these gashes?" I asked.

"Don' rightly know. Maybe with his minin' tools. But seems he was pretty effective," he said. Then he stared over at the hole where Cali's mother had almost fallen through to the basement.

He stepped forward and kicked at the piece of wood Cali and I had examined. We watched him carefully. He reached down and drew his finger along the carved-out line in the board. Then the old man stared up at us.

"What exactly does this Madman of the Mine look like?" Cali asked.

"Well, he's craggy and thin and a bit hunched over from diggin' in the mines. His face is not much to look at and his clothes is tattered—he did go through an explosion. He's kinda spooky lookin', ya know, sorta transparent."

I stammered out, "How do you know what he looks like?"

"The way I heard the tale, some miner was workin'

alone in a tunnel one night. When the fellow started out, he heard something behind him. Turned 'round a coupla times, but there was nothin' ta be seen behind him. He'd almost made it outa the mine before he met up with him.

"The poor guy started ta run, but the Madman of the Mine was fast—still tryin' to hoard the mine for his own. He kept gettin' closer. The miner dodged in and out of the tunnels ta try ta lose the Madman. Reckon that was a dumb move. A phantom hauntin' a mine's gonna know the tunnels better'n anybody. Well, the guy runs smack dab inta a thick wooden door."

I looked at Cali. Her eyes looked as big as mine felt.

Ezra Pike stopped talking for a minute. Then he added softly, "The door was locked."

I concentrated on every word Ezra Pike said. I found myself looking over my shoulder just in case some ghostly miner had snuck up on us.

"Now, the funny thing is where that door was located," Mr. Pike said after another pause.

"Where?" I gulped softly.

"I kin see I'm scarin' you young'ns. Maybe I better just shut my mouth," he said.

"No, please, Mr. Pike. You have to tell us," Cali pleaded.

Finally, Ezra Pike said, "It's in the basement of this very buildin'. Right below where we're standin'."

I scrambled down on my knees and stuck my head through the hole.

"I don't see any door," I said.

"Ya see that basement wall ta the backa the buildin'?" the old caretaker asked.

"No, sir," I answered.

"Well, that's why ya can't see the door. It's in the wall. Back in the dark. Most mines got lotsa tunnels. Some come out under buildings and some come up outa the ground. This one come out right under our feet," Mr. Pike told us.

"What happened to the trapped miner?" Cali wanted to know. "Obviously, if he told people what the Madman looked like, he must have gotten out."

"He clawed at the door. He beat and kicked on it. The mine dweller slowed down a bit because of all the noise. I guess people up here in the store heard all the commotion."

"So they opened the door?" I asked.

Ezra Pike shook his head. "No way."

"Why not?" Cali demanded.

"The good folk of Fearless thought it was the Madman of the Mine tryin' ta get out, and no soul wanted that. And I mean *no* soul. That's why they'd put up that thick door. And that's why they kept it locked *all* the time."

"What about the miner?" I asked.

"Well, he clawed and kicked at that door. He tore his fingernails right off trying ta rip through the wood.

"The Madman was so close, the miner could hear his breathin'. At the last minute someone up here in the store recognized the poor man's voice and reckoned they oughta go down and help him. One brave woman went and unlocked the door.

"She saved that miner's life. The phantom just turned and disappeared into the tunnel. No one's sure why. Maybe the flash of light when the door opened reminded the Madman of the explosion that sentenced him ta the mines forever. The miner lived ta tell everyone what the Madman of the Mine looked like, but he never went back down that hole again."

I glanced over my shoulder at the dim store interior. Then I peered through the hole into the basement again. The old caretaker's story had me totally spooked.

"Knowin' that tale and hearin' about yer mom is what made me come inta the store. I check that door in the basement now and then, just ta make sure it's locked. Just in case the ol' Mad Miner decides ta wander out and claim the mine all over again. I don' wanta be his target."

Cali rubbed her hands together to warm her fingers. I felt the chill in the air as well.

"Why don't you young'ns stay here," Mr. Pike suggested. "It's a might safer. I'll jist go on down there and make sure our friend ain't a roamin' 'round."

Mr. Pike left the plastic bag of trash on the floor and walked toward the stairway to the basement. Then he stopped and gave us a long look.

"From the looks of that there hole, I reckon the Madman's been here at some point. Maybe he thought y'all were after his mine. Then again, he coulda made those cuts years ago. I wish there was some way ta convince him there ain't no silver left," the old caretaker said before he disappeared down the steps.

"Be careful," Cali called after him.

When I thought Mr. Pike was out of earshot, I said to Cali, "I think I'll stay in the little church from now on and pray often—real often." I paused, then asked her, "Do you think there's something to Mr. Pike's story? Or is he just trying to scare us?"

Cali bit her lip and opened her mouth to speak but was interrupted by a horrible yell.

"Help!" It was Ezra Pike. "Help me. He's got me! Hurry! He's gonna drag me inta the mine!"

Cali caught her breath in a single harsh gasp. Without stopping to think about the danger, she started toward the stairway.

I leaped into her way and grabbed her arm. "Cali, we can't just go rushing down there."

"Then what do we do?" she asked.

As I decided how to answer, Mr. Pike's voice cut through the dark one more time. "Hurry, he's got me!" His voice was frantic.

We realized we had no choice. Together we started down the steps into the gloomy basement.

When I spotted Mr. Pike near the bottom of the stairs, his mouth was opened wide, but not in fear. He was laughing.

"Gave you young'ns a right good scare, didn' I?" The caretaker guffawed. "You two oughta see yourselves. Ya look like ya seen a ghost."

"That's not funny," Cali said. "Don't you know it's not right to do things just to frighten people?"

The old man's face sobered up. "You city kids don't do much funnin' 'round, do ya?"

"This is not fun!" Cali said emphatically.

"You young'ns are mighty serious 'bout the Madman." He paused. "An' maybe ya oughta be. Maybe I was wrong ta give ya a fright like that," he confessed.

Cali spun around and stomped up the stairs. I was right behind her, and Ezra Pike followed us. Back upstairs, Mr. Pike scooped up his bag of trash and headed for the door. Just before he left, he turned to us and said, "I shouldn't have joked 'bout the Madman of the Mine. He jist might be inside one of them tunnels, an' there's a lot of them shafts that are open. If'n he's real, he can get out. An' believe me, he won't like all this commotion you church folks is makin'."

The caretaker paused in the doorway to the front porch. He pulled his large red handkerchief from his pocket, cracked it loudly in the air to unfold it, wiped his brow, and left.

Cali and I traded looks.

"How about that?" I asked in an unsteady voice. I realized my hands were shaking.

"He shouldn't have tried to scare us," Cali said. She was still a little angry.

"What if he's telling the truth? What if there really is a phantom Madman of the Mine?" I felt the hairs on the back of my neck tingle. It was all I could do to keep from looking over my shoulder.

"Boone, you don't really believe in ghosts, do you?" Cali asked. "I agree there's something mysterious going on here, and I want to figure out what—before someone gets hurt. The best way to solve a mystery is to add up the clues. But so far, the only real clue we have is a hole in the floor," Cali said.

"Right." I knelt beside the hole and studied the grooves in the broken board again. "Look at how deep these grooves are cut into the wood. And how wide they are."

I put my index finger into one of the grooves. It was at least twice as wide as my finger.

"Should we tell the adults about this?" Cali asked as she studied the groove.

"I'm not sure. All we know is that someone sabotaged the floor, but we don't know when it happened. And we've heard a creepy legend. We don't want them to think we're buying into ghost stories, do we? I think we need to wait until we have more clues about what's going on in Fearless. In the meantime, let's pray for God's guidance and protection," I said.

Cali immediately agreed, and we bowed our heads together. Just as I said, "Amen," I heard, "Frank! Boone! Cali! Where are you?" I recognized Mr. Ramos's voice.

"I hope we're not in trouble for coming back into the store," Cali said nervously.

We quickly started toward the door as I reassured her. "They didn't tell us not to come in here," I reasoned.

"We're over here," Cali called from the doorway. The bright sunlight made her blink.

"Good. You two are accounted for. Have you seen Frank Thomas?" Mr. Ramos asked from across the camp.

"No," I answered. "We finished with the tents. Then we came in here to explore. What's wrong?"

"Mr. Thomas just disappeared. He was going to check on you two and grab a few tools, but that was quite a while ago. It's not like him just to wander off in the middle of a job. And we can't find him anywhere," he told us.

I thought about Mr. Thomas. He was one of the most responsible adults I'd ever met. I couldn't imagine his quitting in the middle of a job.

"Cali and I can check up on the hillside," I suggested. "Maybe he thought he heard us and got hurt looking for us. He could have sprained an ankle or something like that." I was starting to feel a little guilty for not letting anyone know where we'd gone.

"Good idea," Mr. Ramos agreed. He walked off to join the others in searching the buildings.

Cali turned to me. "Where do we start?"

I gestured toward the mountainside behind the little town of Fearless. "That's the most obvious place. We can see across the meadow and down to the dry creek bed from up there."

As we began climbing the steep hillside behind the deserted mining camp, we called out, "Mr. Thomas, can you hear us? Are you hurt? Where are you?"

Suddenly Cali stopped and reached up to twist

the ends of her hair as she frowned in concentration. "Do you remember what Mr. Pike told us about how some of the mine's tunnels open out of the ground? Do you suppose Mr. Thomas decided to explore one?"

"Maybe the Madman of the Mine got him," I added. If the ghostly miner had Mr. Thomas, how would we rescue him?

"I don't believe that story, but I do have a creepy feeling," Cali said.

"What do you mean?" I turned toward her.

"Like someone is watching us. . . . Right now," she added.

Cali was beginning to spook me too. "Let's stick close together," I suggested.

"My thoughts exactly," Cali agreed.

We looked around slowly. Then I saw a tree branch move in a way the wind would never move it.

"Look over there—behind the general store," I whispered.

"Where?"

"See the big old pine tree on the hill? Look at how its lower limbs are moving. What's over there?" I asked.

As I spoke, a figure appeared between the limbs, then vanished. One second it was there. The next it was gone.

"Did you see that?" I questioned.

"It was as if he wanted us to see him for a moment. He caught my eye, then hid," Cali said.

"But who was he?" I asked.

"I don't know. All I could make out was a tattered sleeve." Cali looked at me. Her blue eyes gave away her fear.

I gulped, then whispered, "One thing's for sure, I'm not about to follow him to find out."

"I'm with you on that one," she said. She swiveled her head from side to side, listening. "Did you hear that? Could it be Mr. Thomas? I have a really bad feeling about his disappearing," Cali said.

"Mr. Thomas, can you hear us?" I hollered.

By now we were about halfway up the hill. Cali held up her hand to quiet me.

"Listen," she whispered. She cocked her head to one side and focused her attention.

I heard the sound too. It was muffled, but it sounded like a voice. I couldn't quite make out the words.

"It's Mr. Thomas! But I can't tell where the sound is coming from." Tiny furrows crossed Cali's brow.

"We've got to figure out where Mr. Thomas is. If he's inside the mine somewhere, he could be in danger," I said urgently.

Cali raised her head and called again in a loud voice, "Mr. Thomas, where are you? Mr. Thomas!"

We heard something that sounded like moaning.

"I hope we're not too late," I whispered. "It sounds like he's over there somewhere." I pointed to the right.

"But where?" she asked.

We took a few steps to our right and yelled again. When he answered this time, his voice sounded closer.

"Where are you?" Cali yelled.

Muffled words floated back to us. All I could make out was, "Wooden door."

Cali and I shot a glance at each other. He was trapped in the mine somewhere!

"Mr. Thomas, we're coming!" I yelled.

41

Cali and I anxiously scanned our surroundings. Cali spotted the wooden door in the ground before I did. It was almost hidden in the bushes.

"There it is," she cried. Without waiting for me, she scrambled toward the door.

A heavy wooden plank worked as a lock for the door. It was hinged at one end, and the other end slipped into a piece of metal shaped like the letter *U*.

I quickly lifted the end of the plank from the metal. Cali pulled open the heavy door. An instant later, Mr. Thomas came out, blinking in the daylight.

"Thank the Lord you heard me!" he exclaimed, wiping the back of his hand across his forehead. "I don't think I was in any danger. At least, not right away. Even so, I had started to imagine starving there in the darkness." Then he gave us a wink and a grin. "There's nothing like a good scare to improve your prayer life."

He seemed to be trying to put us at ease. Mr. Thomas taught our Sunday school class. His faith clearly sustained him in his everyday life. I often prayed that I could be more like him.

I smiled back, then peered through the wooden door. "What is this place?" I asked. The door led to a buried room in the side of the mountain. "And why were you up here?"

"I think it's a powder storage vault," Mr. Thomas

explained. "The miners kept blasting caps and dyna-mite in here—away from the town—for safety.

"I came looking for you kids. I was certain I heard a noise up here, and I thought it might have been you. No one answered my call, but I couldn't tell how far back the room went."

Mr. Thomas touched the plank that had locked him inside. "I thought I had braced that board so it would stay up. Guess I was careless. The wind must have blown it down, locking me inside." He stopped and shook his head, then added, "Well, let's get back to the others. It's time to get back to work. Thanks for rescuing me," he added.

As we followed Mr. Thomas back into Camp Fearless, Cali and I traded glances. We had our own ideas about what had lured Mr. Thomas up the hill and how he had been locked inside.

When we reached camp, everyone gathered around us. Mr. Thomas explained what had happened and assured the others that he felt fine. "In fact," he said, "that time alone with God has energized me." He looked around at his friends and announced, "Time to get back to work."

Cali's mom suggested that Cali and I use our energy to gather rocks to build a firepit.

"That sounds like a great idea," I agreed. "I saw lots of flat stones on the hillside. We can also gather wood for tonight's campfire. If this afternoon is any indication, it's going to be pretty cold tonight."

"If we can find some buckets that don't leak, we'll fill them with water. We can use it to drown the fire before we go to bed," Cali added.

"Good idea," Mr. Ramos said. He turned to join Mr. Thomas.

When we were well away from the adults, I quietly said to my friend, "It wasn't the wind that locked Mr. Thomas in."

"No way," Cali agreed quickly. I could tell she'd been thinking about the afternoon as much as I had.

"My guess is the Madman of the Mine saw him go into the powder vault. Then he crept up and used the plank to lock him in." I wrinkled my brow as I thought about what had happened.

"I'm still not convinced there's a ghost in this ghost town," Cali replied. "But I don't think it was an accident that Mr. Thomas got locked in that underground room. I wonder, is someone trying to threaten us?"

We walked a few steps while I digested that idea.

"This place just keeps getting creepier," I finally said. "I feel like we're waiting for something really terrible to happen. In fact, maybe we should call this place Camp Fear instead of Camp Fearless."

"I have the same feeling," Cali said. "We'll just have to keep our eyes open. The adults all seem so excited

44

about turning this place into a church camp that they don't seem to realize that it's really the perfect setting for a spooky movie."

I nodded in agreement as I bent over to pick up a stone from the ground.

We focused on collecting rocks for a while. When we'd brought enough stones into camp, we decided where to place the firepit. Then we dug out a shallow pit, and Cali started building a rock barrier around its edge. I went off in search of water buckets.

I found an old shed and decided it was a likely spot to find buckets. I reached out to push the door open when an eerie feeling struck me. *What if the shed is connected to a mine?* I wondered. *What if the Madman of the Mine is waiting inside?* I cautiously pushed on the door and took a step back. I wanted to peer inside but not be close enough to get captured.

I spotted a couple of old, rusty buckets sitting on what looked like a workbench. There was no ghostly miner waiting for me. I didn't even see a trap door on the floor. The shed looked safe.

I stepped inside and brushed a spider web away from my face. I covered the ground between me and the buckets with two steps.

Suddenly, I froze in my tracks. I heard a rustling noise, just beyond the end of the workbench.

I resisted the urge to turn and dash back into the bright sunlight. Instead I stood motionless with my heart thumping wildly in my chest. *Heavenly Father,* I prayed, *I feel like a real fraidy-cat. I could use an extra shot of courage right now.*

I listened intently, but the noise had stopped. I wondered if I had imagined the noise. I waited in silence for a few more minutes.

More confident now, I reached for the buckets. Then I heard the rustling noise again.

I gasped and jumped back.

As I did, I saw a small gray mouse dash across the floor and vanish through a hole in the shed's floor.

Without stopping to check for other rodents, I grabbed the two buckets and bolted out of the shed into the sunlight. This ghost town was making me nervous.

By the time I got back to Cali, she had finished building the firepit.

"I found these buckets in an old shed," I said triumphantly. There was no reason to tell Cali that a little mouse had frightened me.

"I think there are a couple of buckets in the van too. I'll grab them and meet you by the pump," Cali said.

The old hand pump stood beside the general store. As Mr. Pike had said, the pump worked, but it took a lot of energy.

After we filled the buckets, we set out to gather firewood.

"I don't see any dead trees down here," I said.

"I guess that means we get to climb the hillside again," Cali said with a tight smile. "You know, if we stay here long enough, we're going to turn into mountain goats."

It took us about ten minutes to fill our arms with dry wood. By the time we had it stacked near the firepit, I was puffing.

"How much wood do we need?" I wondered aloud.

"Lots. A campfire can burn wood pretty quickly. Besides, we'll be here tomorrow night as well."

"I guess that means we go back up there again, and again . . ." I gave Cali what I hoped was an encouraging smile.

On our third trip up the hill, a flash of color near the trees caught my attention. I straightened and stared into the woods above us.

"What's wrong?" Cali asked. She stopped picking up wood and looked in the same direction.

"I'm not sure. Something moved up there. I just caught a glimpse of color . . . I think. But I'm really not positive."

I held one hand up to shade my eyes.

Cali stood silently, twisting a lock of her hair with her fingers while she bit her lower lip.

"It may have just been an animal. You know, a sweet, little forest creature out for a romp in the woods." I knew I sounded lame, but I didn't want Cali to be frightened. "I don't see anything now. Most likely, it was my imagination."

"I guess . . . ," Cali agreed. "Think maybe we've got enough wood?" She didn't need to say what we both felt.

I nodded my head and suggested we head back to camp and the company of the adults.

As we turned to leave, thunder came from the hillside above us.

Confused, I looked up. And my breath caught in my throat. Several large rocks were crashing down the steep slope—right toward us.

"Look out, Cali!" I yelled. "It's a rock slide!"

11

Cali looked up at the rocks pounding toward us. In a matter of minutes we could be crushed.

We both dropped our firewood and scrambled out of the path of the rocks. We cowered behind a pine tree as rocks and dirt rolled by. The tree trunk protected us.

"Keep your head down," I cried.

I covered my head with my hands. Cali did the same.

As Mr. Thomas had observed, there's nothing like a good scare to improve your prayer life. *Lord,* I thought, *thank you for this tree that's protecting us. You always know the trouble we'll face, and you have your protection in place for us. All we've got to do is look for it. Help us to see it in every situation. You're awesome, God.*

The slide was over in a few minutes.

As the dust settled, Cali and I lifted our heads.

"Did you see how that started?" I asked with an unsteady voice.

Cali shook her head. "No, but you thought you saw something up there a few minutes ago. Do you think someone started the slide intentionally?"

"It could've just been an accident. Maybe an animal kicked something that triggered it," I said, trying to reassure us both.

I glanced up the mountain. Cali saw my glance and said, "Let's get back to camp. I don't feel safe up here."

I didn't need to be asked twice. We hurried as best we could over the fallen rocks. The sound of the slide had alerted everyone in camp. Mrs. Bittner met us at the edge of the camp looking worried. "I'm so glad to see you two. Are you okay? That slide sounded dangerous."

"We're cool, Mom," Cali answered.

"I'm so glad God protected you. I don't know what I'd do if you two got hurt." Cali's mom reached over and hugged her. Then she said, "I think that's enough foraging for wood for a while. Why don't you focus on setting up camp?"

"Let's find the camp stoves," Cali suggested to me. "There's one in our car. I think Mrs. Williams said there was another in the van."

I checked out the van and found the camp stove. I took it back to where Cali was setting up the one she'd gotten out of her parents' car.

"Here, put that right beside mine. That way we can keep an eye on both of them at once."

50

Cali helped me set up the second camp stove. My lack of camping experience showed as I fumbled with the unfamiliar equipment.

When Cali was satisfied with the cooking arrangements, she suggested we get out the sleeping bags and air mattresses.

Together we located several rolled sleeping bags. There were also air mattresses to be filled.

"Do we have a pump to use on these?" I asked.

"I don't remember seeing one." Cali gave me a quick grin that showed white teeth. "Guess our lungs will have to do the job."

I rummaged in the van again to make sure we hadn't missed any of the sleeping bags. Instead of sleeping gear, I discovered a foot pump. "Hey Cali," I said, holding it up, "Look what I found."

"Wow, Sherlock. Nothing escapes your eagle eye," she joked.

"Cali, can you give us a hand?" Mrs. Bittner called.

"Sure thing, Mom. Be right there." To me she said, "Guess you're on your own. Just don't pump so hard you get muscle cramps."

I gave her a look. Cali giggled and hurried off to help her mother.

As I filled the air mattresses, I studied the area around me. The grassy meadow was off to my right. The church and most of the old mining town lay behind me. To my left was the general store. And

Library
Campbell Church of Christ

ahead of me was the edge of the woods. I felt a shiver as I stared at the trees.

A few moments later, I saw the presence I'd felt. A tattered sleeve fluttering in the wind caught my attention. When I looked up higher, I saw a terrible face.

It's the Madman of the Mine! My brain screamed at me. *Lord, help!*

"Hey, look over there!" One of the men shouted from near the church.

I spun around, startled. Had someone else seen the ghost?

"Wow, look at the size of that elk! Quick, before it gets across the meadow. What a beautiful sight."

They hadn't seen the Madman. In fact, no one was even looking my way. I turned back toward where I'd seen the tattered sleeve and disfigured face. All I saw were placid trees. I looked to my left and then to my right. I squinted into the shaded tree line. The ghostly figure had vanished.

I stood deep in thought, trying to figure out what I might have seen. I didn't even notice when Cali returned.

"Hey, what spooked you?" she asked. "You look as though you just saw a ghost."

"Hmm. Maybe I did," I answered. I told her about the creepy face I'd seen.

"Just because you saw an unusual face doesn't mean you saw the Madman of the Mine. I wonder if many people come up here. Maybe you saw a hiker out there," Cali suggested. "Or someone from the ski resort. Is it possible the shadows from the trees just made the face look disfigured?"

I bit my lip as I thought about her question. I had to laugh at myself when I realized I had picked up Cali's nervous habit. Next, I'd be twirling my hair. "I suppose it's possible," I answered. "The only one who could really tell us whether many people come up here is Mr. Pike, the caretaker."

"That man gives me the creeps," Cali said, shuddering.

"But he's the only one who would know. His cabin is across the dry creek bed," I said. "At least, that's what he told Mr. Ramos and me when we arrived. Do we have time to talk to him before supper?"

"I'll check with Mom," Cali said.

She ran toward the adults and said, "Mom, Boone and I have something we need to ask the caretaker. His cabin is just across the creek bed. Can we go before supper?"

"We're planning on quitting here soon. I expect we'll be ready to eat in about an hour," Mrs. Bittner replied. "Just be back by then."

Before she even got out the words, "Thanks, Mom," Cali began running back toward me. Seconds later we were both headed toward the caretaker's cabin.

"I'll bet this path leads to the cabin," Cali said after we crossed the dry creek.

We started along the path at a trot. In spite of myself, I glanced over my shoulder several times. Beautiful white trees lined the path. To distract myself, I asked Cali if she knew their name.

"Aspen." Cali said simply.

"I thought Aspen was a town with a ski resort . . ." I joked. She just shook her head.

Then she looked excited. "I think I see the cabin—up ahead, off to the left. Just past this grove of trees."

We slowed our pace to a quick walk. I kept glancing to both sides of the path. I didn't want to seem like a wimp, but the lack of bright sunlight bothered me. The feeling that something was about to reach out and grab me kept me alert.

"Ohhh."

Cali skidded to a stop. I almost ran into her.

Cali turned toward me. "Did you hear that?" she whispered.

"Ohhhhhhhh." It was a long moan, full of pain and suffering.

I swallowed.

"Ohhhhhhh."

"Do you think it's the ghost?" I asked, also whispering.

"Ohhhhhhhhhh."

Cali had to wet her lips before she said, "It could be a trick."

I prayed that she was right. Then I called out, "Who's there?"

The moaning got louder.

13

I gathered my courage and called out again, "Who's there?"

"It's Mr. Pike. Who in tarnation do ya think would be out here?" The old man's tone was unpleasant.

"What's the matter?" called Cali.

"I took me a shortcut from my cabin. I slipped on a loose stone and twisted my ankle like a dumb horse would. I'd be much obliged if you two would come here and give me a helpin' hand."

Well, I figured, *we had come looking for Mr. Pike, and we couldn't just leave him in the woods with a sprained ankle.* I looked at the dense trees and swallowed my fear that something was lurking in there.

"Where are you, Mr. Pike?" Cali called.

"I'm 'bout a stone's throw off the path. Keep on movin' a bit farther and look ta yer left. And make it snappy; my ankle hurts somethin' fierce."

Cali and I traded glances as we followed the caretaker's directions.

Sure enough, just seconds later we saw Mr. Pike. He made it easy for us to spot him by waving his red bandanna.

"Durn fool thing I did," the old caretaker said with a shake of his head. "Long as I lived here, I've known that it's a might tricky walkin' off the paths. Lotta good knowin' does a fella. Knowin' ain't enough. Ya gotta steer clear of dangerous places like that." He waved his hand at the jumbled rocks around him. "Now, did I listen to my own advice? Not on yer life. Here, give me a hand, kids."

Together Cali and I helped the injured man to his feet. He groaned when the foot of his hurt ankle touched the ground. He then wiped his brow with his red handkerchief.

"Do you need a doctor?" Cali asked with concern.

"No, but I could use me a helpin' hand back to my cabin. Once I'm inside I'll be fine. I'll soak the ankle, wrap it, and put the old foot up in the air for a spell."

He leaned heavily on my shoulder as we started toward his cabin. Cali reached down and picked up the old man's pack before following us. Luckily it was only a short distance to the cabin.

"I can manage now," Mr. Pike said when we reached his door. "I'm right thankful fer yer help."

"Are you certain you're okay?" Cali asked as she handed him his pack.

"I said I was, didn' I?" His tone was sharp again. The old man set his lips in a grim expression. "Sorry,

I didn't mean ta bite yer head off. Right now, I jist want ta get inside and get off this here swellin' ankle." The caretaker went inside and closed the door before either Cali or I could say another word.

For several seconds, we stared at the door, dumbfounded. Finally I whispered, "Do you think I should knock?"

"He's clearly in pain and in no mood for conversation," Cali whispered in reply. "We'll have to come back tomorrow, when he's feeling better, to ask him about hikers."

We reluctantly turned around and walked away from the cabin.

"Did you find the caretaker?" Mrs. Bittner asked.

"We did. And it's a lucky thing we went looking for him when we did," Cali told her mother.

"He took a shortcut through the aspen grove." I picked up the story. "But he slipped and twisted his ankle."

"Oh, the poor man," Mrs. Bittner said in concern. "Does he need a doctor?"

"He said no. He'd rather just soak and elevate it," Cali told her mother.

"Well, I'm sure he's in no shape to cook his own dinner. Your dad and I can take a plate of food to him this evening."

"That's a nice idea, Mrs. Bittner," I told her. "How about if I take it to him, since I know the way?" I saw this as my chance to question the caretaker about possible hikers in the area.

After dinner, I took the plate of food the Bittners had prepared and set out for the caretaker's cabin.

It wasn't until I entered the aspen grove that I began to feel worried. Without thinking about it, I checked over my shoulder. Everything seemed mighty quiet. I wondered why that didn't put me at ease.

I was almost certain the Madman of the Mine wasn't waiting for me among the aspen trees. Almost. But not quite.

The sound of a branch breaking caused me to freeze. I listened intently. Was something moving just off to my right, among the trees?

I bit down on my lower lip. There were no more sounds. I tried to convince myself that I'd heard an animal. To calm down, I prayed. *Lord, I know I'm in the woods, and lots of real creatures make their homes here. Help me to remember that their sounds are natural. Please be with me as I deliver dinner to Mr. Pike. I know you'll keep me safe. Thank you.*

I took a step forward. Then another.

Again I heard something off to my right. To prove to myself I was being silly, I looked over to see what animal had made the noise.

All I could see were moving shadows.

What was out there?

I walked stealthily forward, stopping every few feet to listen and peer into the grove of trees.

I drew in a deep breath of relief when I saw the cabin just ahead.

I knocked on the cabin's faded door and stepped back to wait. I expected Mr. Pike to take awhile to hobble to the door. But the door opened almost at once.

"What's that yer aholdin' there, young man?" Mr. Pike asked suspiciously.

"The Bittners sent you some dinner," I explained politely.

The caretaker looked puzzled. "Why in tarnation would they do somethin' like that?" he asked.

"They thought you might not be able to cook because of your sprained . . . ankle."

As I spoke I glanced at Mr. Pike's ankle. He seemed to be putting weight on both feet.

"Oh yeah, yeah, my ankle," he stammered. "It seems ta be afeelin' a sight better. I just soaked it for a bit and put it up in the air for a spell. Healed it up real quick." Mr. Pike reached for the plate. "Be sure ta tell them that I'm much obliged. I'll return the plate washed up and clean."

"Oh, one of us can pick it up tomorrow," I said quickly. "There's no need for you to walk all that way on a sore ankle."

"It'd probably do the old foot good ta do some walkin' on it. I was already plannin' ta come on down and join you folk a little later."

"Uh . . . Mr. Pike, there's something I'd like to ask you," I said meekly.

"Well, speak up," the caretaker replied. When I hesitated, he asked, "Cat got yer tongue?"

"Well, I was just wondering, do many people come up here to hike around?"

The caretaker rubbed his whiskered chin with his rough hands and stared at me for several moments before replying, "Almost never, on account of the Madman of the Mine. 'Most ever'one knows 'bout it. Why ya askin'? Did ya see something?" Ezra Pike poked for an answer.

I explained what I had seen and heard that afternoon.

"I reckon it could be a hiker . . . ," Mr. Pike said. "But then again, maybe our old friend from the mine found a way out. I've been lucky so far. The ol' miner hasn't come after me. But from what you've told me, you might not be so lucky."

I gulped. My throat suddenly felt dry.

"Ya better be arunnin' on back to yer camp now. But ya oughta be a might bit careful." The caretaker closed the door following his warning.

Nervously, I turned to retrace my steps down the trail. When I entered the aspens again, I glanced over my shoulder. Something was watching me. I could feel it. Then I saw a curtain at one of the cabin's windows move.

Was the caretaker taking care of me or was he making sure that some mythical Mad Miner took care of me? Or had the breeze simply tossed the light material as it blew through the open window?

I set off rapidly through the trees.

Was it possible for a sprained ankle to get better so quickly? I wondered. Of course it might not have been injured as badly as Mr. Pike had first thought. But even so, it seemed to have healed too fast. It hadn't even looked swollen. But what did I know about sprained ankles other than that they hurt?

The trail seemed spookier than ever in the growing darkness. I tried to hurry, but I was afraid of losing my way. If I veered off into the woods, I might never find camp again.

I began to wish I'd remembered a flashlight. I glanced toward the west. The sun's glow was barely visible above the mountains. Soon I'd have trouble seeing.

Then I forgot about the approaching darkness. I

forgot about possibly losing my way. I forgot about everything but my fear. What was that noise? I stood still in the middle of the trail and strained to hear.

Somewhere near the end of the aspen grove something made a faint snapping sound. I knew at once that it was a dry branch. Someone or something had stepped on it. Another branch snapped, louder. Whatever it was, it was moving toward me.

Only one thought filled my mind.

The Madman of the Mine had come looking for me.

Dear Lord, why didn't I bring a flashlight? Please guide me safely back to camp. Be a lamp for my feet, like the Bible says.

I heard a rustling sound. Another stick snapped. It was almost in front of me.

My heart pounded so loudly I was afraid it would give me away. I knew something was out there, waiting for me, ready to grab me before I got back to camp.

I thought about racing back to Mr. Pike's cabin. I wondered if I could slip off the trail without getting lost as I toyed with the idea of sneaking up on the Madman of the Mine. Maybe, if I could get a good look at him, I could solve this mystery.

Then I realized I had to run for my life. It was my only hope. I spun around, ready to race back down the trail.

"Boone, is that you?"

I stopped. The voice sounded familiar.

"Boone!"

The beam of a flashlight suddenly glowed brightly. Cali waved the beam around trying to find me. *Thank you, Lord. You are a lamp for my feet.*

"Here I am." I called out. I hoped my voice didn't sound as shaky as I felt.

"When it started to get dark, we realized you didn't have a flashlight. We had visions of you falling in the aspen grove in the dark. Since Mr. Pike fell and twisted his ankle in the daylight, I figured nighttime would be really dangerous," Cali said.

"Thanks. I'm really glad you came to meet me." She flashed me a smile.

When we emerged from the grove of trees, I could see the bright glow of the campfire ahead. It seemed to welcome me back from my short journey.

"Did you ask Mr. Pike if people come up here to hike very often?" Cali inquired.

"I asked him, but he said they were pretty rare. The legend of the Madman of the Mine keeps them away. Then he warned me to be careful."

Cali shivered and changed the subject. "While you were gone, I asked Mr. Ramos why Fearless was deserted," she said. "I wanted to see how different his story would be from Mr. Pike's."

I stopped walking. "What did he say?"

Cali stopped and played the beam of her flashlight over the stones near our feet.

"He told me the silver mine ran dry years ago. When that happened, the people left. He said it's not unusual for mining camps and towns to be abandoned almost overnight."

She was quiet for a moment, then she said, "I think I'm beginning to figure this mystery out."

"Really? Let me in on it," I requested.

"All this has something to do with the silver mine," she told me.

"Wow, Sherlock. How did you figure that out?" I asked, rolling my eyes.

"No. Seriously," she said.

I furrowed my brows in a question. She could see she had my attention, so she went on.

"Somebody wants Camp Fearless to fail. I think it's because that somebody doesn't want us poking around in the mine. There's something about that hole in the ground. Something worth scaring us away," she said.

"Like what?" I asked.

"Silver," she whispered. "There must still be silver in the mine. And there's only one thing we can do."

"I don't think I want to hear this," I said dubiously.

"We have to go into the mine and find out what someone is trying to protect," she stated. I gulped and didn't say anything for a few seconds.

"Okay, how do we do that?" I finally asked.

"I don't know, but between the two of us we can figure it out," she replied. "Let's think about it on our way back to camp."

We had only walked another hundred yards or so when a terrible wail filled the air.

It began as a quiet moan and turned into a high-pitched scream.

I felt the back of my neck prickle. I strained to see something, anything, through the darkness.

16

"What was that?" My teeth threatened to chatter.

Cali flashed the light in the direction of the sound. "Coyotes," she said. "I've heard them on other camping trips."

She didn't seem scared by the coyotes, so I forced myself to breathe deeply. I quietly followed her toward camp. But several times I turned back to the sound of the wailing coyotes.

Cali broke our silence with a startled, "Oh!" When she saw that I jumped in response, she quickly added, "I almost forgot. I promised that we'd bring sticks for toasting marshmallows."

She pulled a folded camping knife out of her pocket and held it up for me to see. "We can cut some green branches with this. Here, take the flashlight and shine it on these bushes. The long, thin branches should make great marshmallow sticks."

I held the flashlight as Cali cut a half dozen branches from a bush. She trimmed smaller twigs from the branches to make them easier to carry back to camp.

"There," she said as she got to her feet. With the skill of an accomplished camper, she easily folded the blade back into the knife and slipped it in to her pocket. "That should do it."

"I'm ready to go back to the fire," I admitted. "Those coyotes are giving me the creeps."

Cali carried the marshmallow sticks, and I led the way with the light. A cloud moved across the moon, and suddenly the dark night became almost black.

A few steps later, Cali reached forward and grabbed me.

"Do you hear that?" she whispered.

I froze at the sound of her question. I listened hard. But all I heard was a lone coyote still yipping sharply in the distance. And the murmur of voices from camp.

I shook my head as I whispered back, "No. What did you think you heard?"

"Listen." Cali spoke so softly that I could barely hear her. I strained to pay attention.

I felt it before I heard it. The faintest sound followed a moment later. Was someone trying to sneak up on us?

Cali shivered. I knew that in the darkness beside me she was biting on her bottom lip. She was also probably playing with a little piece of hair.

The sound got louder. Something was definitely shuffling through the grass toward us.

I wished with all my might that the night weren't so black.

Cautiously, I swung the light in a half circle around us.

Cali cried out in surprise.

"What is that?" I asked as I tried to make out what the light beam had centered on.

"It's a porcupine." Cali replied, sounding relieved.

I couldn't see what she was relieved about. Didn't porcupines shoot quills at people?

I watched the slow-moving creature warily. It appeared undisturbed by either us or the light. It waddled several feet along the trail and then turned. I let the beam follow the animal into the brush beside the trail.

"Its a good thing neither of us stumbled into him. If we had, we'd be picking quills out of our legs all night," Cali told me. "Dad says a porcupine won't pick a fight, but it won't back away from one either."

"And if we'd bumped into it, the porcupine would have figured that we wanted to fight."

"That's about it."

I shined the light on the animal one last time. Then with the beam pointed at the trail ahead, we started forward again.

"I have to admit I still feel uneasy out here," Cali told me. "Part of it is being in the mountains—and that it's so dark." She paused.

I finished for her. "And some of it has to do with Camp Fearless. So far its name doesn't seem to fit."

When we reached the campfire, I spotted Ezra Pike.

"Look who's here," I hissed to Cali. "How did he get here without us seeing him?"

"There must be another trail. And he didn't take the time to stop for marshmallow sticks," she whispered back. "I guess he didn't take long to eat the dinner you took him. Boy, his hurt ankle sure got well in a hurry."

Mrs. Williams had the group's attention. She was explaining how we could rig up a temporary shower.

When the others greeted the idea with enthusiasm, she led a small group away to show them some likely locations. Mr. Ramos noticed us and said, "There you are! We were beginning to wonder if some creature in the woods got in your way." He chuckled at the idea. "Come on over to the fire. I want to see how well those marshmallow sticks work."

Cali handed him one. Then she and I each stuck a marshmallow on the end of a stick.

As we held our sticks over the fire, Mrs. Williams and the others returned. They must have made a decision on where to set up the shower because she was proposing another idea. "I've been looking at the slope to the west of Camp Fearless. It would make a perfect sled run if we opened the camp during the winter."

"I wonder why the Atlas Ski Resort didn't try to buy this land from Mr. Markham," Cali mused. "This area would be a perfect addition to their resort."

Before I could reply, Mr. Pike interrupted in a low voice, "See that big tree nex' ta the old blacksmith shop?" He pointed into the darkness. "Ya can jist see its outline now that the moon's acomin' out from behin' the clouds." He paused and pulled out his red handkerchief, snapped it in the air, and then wiped soot off his fingers.

I strained to see. "To the right of that building?"

"That's the one, young man. The people of Fearless called it the Hangin' Tree."

Suddenly I sensed danger.

"Them folk that broke the law got hanged on that tree. Hanged by the neck, doin' a little dance, until they was dead," Mr. Pike continued dramatically.

I felt my eyes open wide in surprise. "Um, how many people were hanged on that tree?" I asked in a shaky voice.

"Boone, your marshmallow!" Cali gave me a dig with her elbow.

Too late, I pulled my flaming marshmallow away from the fire. As I blew out my dessert, the old caretaker said, "Ta answer yer question, young man, I

75

don' reckon as anybody 'round these parts knows. My guess would be a dozen or so. There was a lot of crime in these minin' towns then. People stole. Some drank too much and killed. That sort of thing.

"I've heard tell that the spirits of them that was hanged on the Hangin' Tree still roam 'round here at night. Ya might say that this is one ghost town with real ghosts." Mr. Pike stared into the coals of the campfire.

I bit into my crispy marshmallow. I barely even noticed how hot it still was.

"Fact is," Ezra Pike continued, "some people swear as how they seen the ghosts of men still adanglin' from that tree. Mostly on dark nights like this. If ya happen to look at the right moment, ya might jist see one of those boys still kickin' away."

"I think, Mr. Pike, that we've had enough ghost stories for tonight," Mrs. Bittner said sharply.

"You're right, of course, ma'am," Mr. Pike said as he got to his feet. "Thanks for the dinner. It was right neighborly of ya ta think of me."

"It was our pleasure," Cali's mom said.

"Time for me to git on back home." Mr. Pike switched on his powerful flashlight as he spoke.

He swung the bright beam in an arc around the fire. The yellow circle of light swept over the front of the general store. It traveled down the main street of Fearless. Then, just for an instant, Mr. Pike let the beam of light rise to the Hanging Tree.

"Oh!" I gasped.

But the light beam moved on before I was sure what I'd seen.

"Shine your light back on the Hanging Tree!" I almost shouted.

"What?" Mr. Pike turned toward me.

"Please shine your light on the Hanging Tree. I'm sure I saw something dangling from one of the branches!"

18

"What did you see, Boone?" Cali leaned forward to stare toward the tree. I looked in her direction and noticed Mrs. Bittner frowning beside her.

"When the light struck the tree, I think I saw something hanging from it."

Mr. Pike directed the powerful beam of light back to the trunk of the old tree. Then he moved it slowly toward its top.

"More to the right," I told him. "Shine it on that first big branch on the right."

The old caretaker did as I asked. When he got the light centered on the branch, we saw nothing there.

"That the branch, young man?" Mr. Pike asked.

"That's the one," I had to answer, but I had trouble getting the words out. I knew everyone around the campfire was staring at me.

"I don't see anything hanging from that branch," Mr. Ramos pointed out.

"I don't either," I admitted. "Not now. But there was just a minute ago. I saw it. I really did."

"At least you thought you did," Mr. Ramos said gently. "Sometimes your imagination can play tricks on you—especially if you expect to see something."

I nodded and stared at the ground, scuffing the toe of my sneaker in the dirt. I was sure I had seen something in the Hanging Tree.

"Here." Cali handed me a fresh marshmallow with a sympathetic smile. "Let's toast some more of these."

"Sure." I realized Cali was trying to say that she believed I had seen something, even if no one else saw it. And she was taking the spotlight off me.

"I'm sorry. Truly I am," Mr. Pike said. "I didn't mean ta scare the boy. I was jist tryin' ta give you folks a tiny taste of what Fearless is all about." Mr. Pike turned away from the fire. Then with his powerful light leading the way, he started off toward his cabin. I noticed that he didn't seem to be limping at all.

I ate another marshmallow without really tasting it. I wanted to go check out the Hanging Tree, but what was the use? I quietly wandered away from the fire, thinking about Camp Fearless.

A few minutes later, Cali joined me. Together we stared at the Hanging Tree.

"I saw it too," Cali said in a low voice.

"You did?" I turned to peer at her in the dark.

"I'm sure I saw something dangling just where you said it was. But I only saw it for an instant. When the light moved past, I wondered if maybe I'd imagined it. But then you cried out, and I knew I hadn't."

"Why didn't you say something?" I demanded.

"Because I was too busy wondering why the adults missed it."

"Probably because they weren't looking. You and I were the only ones really interested," I answered.

"I think the Hanging Tree fits into this mystery somehow," Cali said.

"How?" I asked.

"I'm not sure yet. But I wonder why the figure appeared just when Mr. Pike flashed his light on it," she mused.

"That's a good question. And how does the tree tie into the mine?" I asked her.

Cali's mom interrupted our conversation by calling out, "Hey everybody, come on back to the fire for some hot chocolate." When we joined the adults, we discovered Mrs. Bittner had already measured the cocoa into cups. Water was just coming to a boil over the fire.

By the time I had finished my hot chocolate, I realized how sleepy I was.

"I don't know about the rest of you, but I'm beat," Mr. Thomas announced as he covered a yawn with his fist.

Everyone agreed that hitting the sleeping bags sounded like a good idea. Before we went to our tents, I helped Mr. Ramos drown the fire. First we slowly poured a full bucket of water onto the fire, and I stirred the coals with a stick. Then we added a second bucket of water. This time, Mr. Ramos stirred up the coals, looking for any live embers.

Just to be safe, I poured on the contents of a third bucket onto the black coals. Steam rose from our firepit but no smoke.

"That should do it," Mr. Ramos said. "Time for bed."

As I trudged tiredly toward bed, I looked back at the Hanging Tree. The moon had risen higher and provided more light than it had before. I could clearly see that nothing was hanging from the tree.

So why did I still have the creepy feeling that danger lurked in Camp Fearless? Was my imagination just working overtime? I didn't think so.

Maybe we weren't really in danger, but I knew deep in my bones that there was something mysterious going on here. Something mysterious that Cali and I would get to the bottom of.

I crawled into my sleeping bag. I lay silently for a moment, intending to listen for noises. But, overcome with exhaustion, I fell asleep almost immediately.

Later—I have no idea how much later—I had a terrible dream: someone was screaming at me.

Someone was trapped in a burning building. I had to rescue him. But I didn't know how.

Suddenly I sat up in my sleeping bag.

"Fire!" a man's voice yelled. "Everyone up! Out of your tents! Camp Fearless is on fire!"

19

I scrambled out of my sleeping bag. Mr. Ramos was already up and unzipping our tent flap.

"Hurry! We need everyone out here to help!" Someone yelled loudly.

"Oh no! The fire's at the church!" I recognized Mrs. Bittner's voice.

I jumped into my clothing as quickly as I could. Then I raced out of the tent after Mr. Ramos.

All around me, I saw people running toward the church. I followed as fast as I could.

Though it was the middle of the night, the moon gave us enough light to see. And ahead of us, the fire glowed yellow and red in the night.

"Buckets!" someone called out. "We need buckets to carry water."

I stopped almost in mid-stride. The buckets were back by the firepit.

"Someone help me grab the buckets," I called out. Then, running as fast as I'd ever run in my life, I headed for the remains of our campfire.

"I'll help you, Boone," Cali volunteered. She had been right behind me.

The next few minutes were a blur in my mind. I gathered up the buckets we had used earlier. Cali snagged two more from the van. Together we ran to the old water pump where Mr. Ramos was waiting. He jerked the iron handle up and down.

It seemed to take forever to fill the first bucket. Someone, maybe it was Mr. Foster, grabbed the bucket of water and hurried off toward the blaze.

Cali and I took turns with the adults, pumping furiously to fill the buckets with water and running with them to save the church building. Then we ran back to the pump for refills. I lost count of how many times we filled the buckets and ran that loop.

Just as I wondered how long I could keep going, a cheer rose from the church.

"It sounds like the fire's out," Cali said with a sigh as she sat on the ground for a much-deserved rest.

"Let's go see how much damage it did," I suggested.

Together we took another, slower trip toward the church. The beams of half a dozen flashlights darted about.

The smell of smoke filled the air. I could hear the hissing sound of steam escaping from the doused fire.

"How badly is the church damaged?" Cali asked after we got closer to the others.

"Happily, not at all," Mr. Ramos answered. "All that burned was a pile of wood and garbage beside the church. Some of that woodpile has been sitting around for years, so the wood was extremely dry. We're lucky the whole church didn't go up in flames."

"How did the fire start?" I forgot about how tired my arms were. I suddenly realized that the fire might be another important clue.

"We don't know," Cali's mom said. "None of us smoke. And the only fire we had was our campfire. But you and Mr. Ramos drowned that before we went to bed."

"Maybe a spark from our campfire blew this far earlier in the evening." I could tell Cali was trying to make sense out of this mystery too.

"That doesn't seem very likely," Mrs. Bittner replied. "There was just a slight breeze this evening. And even if a spark had blown this far, the fire would have started at once. The woodpile was totally dry and ready to burn. It doesn't make sense that the fire would have taken so long to start. No, I don't think it was a spark."

Cali touched my arm with the tips of her fingers. I turned toward her. Moonlight illuminated her face. She raised her eyebrows in a silent question.

I shrugged my shoulders. Her mom had confirmed what I felt. This wasn't an accident. Was it the Madman of the Mine? But if he wanted to drive us away from Camp Fearless, why didn't he set the church on fire?

Cali suddenly stiffened. I watched her eyes widen.

"What is it?"

"Behind you. Something's moving in the dark. It's coming closer."

"What's going on here?" The beam from the care-taker's powerful light came on. It swept past me and Cali then settled on Mr. Ramos.

"We just put out a fire," Mr. Ramos answered calmly. "An old woodpile caught fire."

Mr. Pike walked closer to inspect the smoldering rubble.

"If you folk are goin' ta turn this place into a camp for the young'ns, ya better be more careful," the older man said sharply. "These here buildin's are as dry as bones. Yer lucky it weren't a lot worse fer ya. Ya foolish bunch of city folk coulda burned up all of Fearless."

His flashlight swept over the blackened pile. Steam still rose from the pieces of wood. Then he turned slowly and let the beam of his light play over each of us. "A fire could kill an entire camp fulla young'ns," he told us. "Keep that in mind the nex' time yer feelin' careless." He shook his head in disgust. Muttering something else half under his breath, he pulled his handkerchief from his pocket, snapped it in the air to unfold it, then cleaned the lens of his flashlight. Then without waiting for anyone to respond to his reprimand, Mr. Pike turned and walked back toward his cabin.

Two of the men carried empty buckets toward the pump. They wanted some clean water to wash the soot and sweat from their hands and faces.

After we all cleaned up, Mrs. Bittner reminded us, "It's late. Let's try to get some sleep. We still have a full day ahead of us." Slowly we all walked back toward our tents.

I leaned my head close to Cali so no one else could hear our conversation. "It was the Madman of the Mine. I just know he's behind this," I told her.

"I'm not convinced," she answered. "I want to get a better look at some of our clues tomorrow morning."

I thought about her skepticism as we walked the rest of the way to her tent in silence. I went over the day's events. I was missing something. Was the Mad Miner involved? Somewhere during the day, I had run across the one clue I needed to solve this whole thing, but I couldn't think of what it was.

"See you in the morning," Cali said, waking me from my reverie. She turned to duck into her tent but stopped and reached out to me. "You know what we have to do tomorrow?" she asked.

"I know—we have to check out the mine. It looks like it's up to us to make sure the camp will be safe for kids," I answered. She nodded and slipped inside her tent. I turned toward mine.

Even after Mr. Ramos came in and got settled, I couldn't go back to sleep. I lay in the dark wondering about the future of Camp Fearless.

Lord, I want to thank you for protecting us and the church building from the fire. I need some guidance right now. Show me what Cali and I should do next. When we go into the mine tomorrow, Lord, please watch over us and keep us safe. Thank you, Father. Amen.

Finally I drifted off.

For the second time that night I was startled from a sound sleep. What woke me this time? Was there something near the tent? I lay motionless and listened.

But all I heard was the wind in the trees. Had something in my dreams startled me?

No. Now I heard it—outside the tent. But what was it?

The nylon tent wall wouldn't be much protection from the Madman of the Mine. Not if he wanted to rip open the tent and grab me.

Should I get out of my sleeping bag? Wake Mr. Ramos? Try to escape?

The sound came again—right on the other side of the tent wall. The Madman had come for me.

"Get out of here!" Mr. Thomas yelled into the night.

"We should have locked the food in the van." That sounded like Mr. Bittner. "Raccoons will tear into anything we leave out."

Someone banged on a metal pot. Someone else laughed and commented that our camping skills seemed a little rusty.

"Quite a night, isn't it?" Mr. Ramos had sat up in his sleeping bag.

"It sure is." I tried to sound as though I had not been frightened.

"I guess those raccoons were having quite a feast." Mr. Ramos chuckled and lay back down. Moments later his deep breathing told me he had gone back to sleep.

I tried to relax and let sleep claim me too. Part of my mind kept going back to how my heart had hammered when I awoke only minutes before.

The presence of the Mad Miner had seemed so

real. But it wasn't. Maybe my other feelings were exaggerated as well. As hard as I tried to convince myself otherwise, part of me still believed that there was something waiting for me out there.

The rest of the camp had returned to silence. I wondered how long I'd been awake. Then I heard another sound outside. I strained to figure out what it was. I even sat up in my sleeping bag and pressed my ear to the side of the tent.

I took a deep, calming breath. That long, drawn out "whooing" had to be an owl. Didn't it? Then I wondered what sort of sound the ghost of a miner would make. The thought almost made me laugh at myself.

A large shadow moved across one side of the tent. With it came an uneven shuffling sound. Then it was gone.

I tried to convince myself it was just one of the adults in our group. But I hadn't heard anyone open a tent. Besides, I'd never heard anyone walk with such a strange gait.

I had to see who it was.

With my heart in my throat, I crawled toward my tent door. Carefully, silently, I unzipped the flap. Then, crouching in the tent's opening, I peered out.

The owl hooted again from the top of a nearby tree.

Then I saw it. Movement in the shadows beside the van. It was too far away to make out what it was. But I could tell that shadow was no raccoon!

I crouched absolutely still for what seemed like hours. The owl hooted one more time. Then a cloud covered the moon, and all the shadows melted together.

With nothing left to see, I zipped the tent flap again and crawled back into my sleeping bag. I decided I couldn't go back to sleep. I had to stay awake and listen.

Despite my efforts to stay awake, the next thing I knew, the sun was shining on the tent. I had dozed off sometime during the night. Outside I heard the voices of the other campers.

I checked my watch. It was not quite seven-thirty. Already most of the group seemed up and ready for the day.

To my surprise I discovered that Mr. Ramos had left the tent without waking me. Moving quickly, I dressed and scrambled out into the bright morning.

Cali's parents had already started breakfast. I spotted Cali pouring coffee for Mr. Thomas.

"Nice of you to rise and shine, Boone," Cali teased when she saw me.

"Guess I slept in a little," I admitted.

"Grab a plate and have something to eat," Mr. Thomas urged me. "We have a big day ahead of us."

As we ate, the adults talked a bit about last night's experience. Then they began to plan the day. There was even more work to do than we'd expected because of the fire. We decided to start the day with a short devotional and prayers of thanksgiving and praise to God that we'd doused the fire without anyone getting hurt.

After our final "Amen," Mrs. Williams said, "I'd like to see if I can rig up that shower we talked about yesterday. We'll have to make do with cold water to begin with, but I've got some ideas about mixing in hot water later."

"That sounds like a good place to start," Mr. Ramos agreed.

"I'll give you a hand," Mr. Thomas offered.

As the adults split up to start their various tasks, Cali and I cleaned up the breakfast dishes. The last things we tackled were the pots and pans.

After the last pot was dried and stacked, Cali led me toward the old general store. I threw her a questioning glance, and she gave me a quick nod in response. I drew a deep breath. We had to go in.

When we neared the store, we found several adults on the front porch. We'd have to wait a bit to explore the mine. Instead, I called to Mr. Ramos, "We want to check out the floor where Mrs. Bittner fell through. Want to join us?"

He raised his eyebrows. Then he nodded. "Sure thing, Boone. Let's give it a good look."

We left the other adults outside, discussing how to

get more light into the old store. Mr. Ramos followed Cali and me to the hole in the floor.

Cali picked up one of the pieces of wood that had broken off when we'd rescued her mother. She held it so Mr. Ramos could see the deep grooves dug into the wood.

"Could those grooves have been made by a pickax?" I watched Mr. Ramos's expression as I asked the question.

"You mean like someone deliberately weakened the floor?" He held the board up and studied it.

"Right." I hesitated.

Mr. Ramos lowered the wood to look at me. Then he held the board up again and squinted.

"Let's go outside where the light's better," I suggested.

We walked out onto the porch.

"I won't say these marks weren't made deliberately," Mr. Ramos said after studying them carefully. "It seems unlikely that someone tried to sabotage the floor, however. Someone would have had to reach all the way up from the basement floor to do this, and that's a pretty long reach. Anyway, whatever cut these gashes did so a long time ago," he added.

Mr. Ramos held one of the boards toward me. Cali and I looked at the board, then at each other.

I felt confused. These grooves and cuts were dark, as if they'd been exposed to air for a long time. They did look old.

One of the other adults asked Mr. Ramos a question.

"Time for me to get back to work," he said. He handed the broken floorboard to me and walked into the store with the rest of his work group.

Cali looked at me. "Those grooves were fresh yesterday. The wood looked bright and yellow."

"I know. It doesn't make sense." I stared at the broken floorboard in my hand. "But then nothing here seems to make sense."

I watched Cali's face. I could see she was connecting some of the clues. She kept looking from the broken board to the woods beyond our tents.

"Hey, Boone, can you come give us a hand?" Mr. Foster called.

"Sure," I called back. I left Cali alone on the porch deep in thought.

I helped the adults tear up the damaged flooring. After a while, Cali came inside and helped Mr. Ramos measure for new, larger windows to let in more light.

I heard someone mention that it would soon be time for lunch. Surprised, I checked my watch and could not believe it was nearly half-past eleven. Time really slips by quickly when you're deep into a project.

I discovered that I suddenly felt hungry. But that

thought flew from my mind when I heard a strange sound in the basement. My heart began to beat faster. Straining to hear, I glanced toward Cali.

She was holding a board in place for Mr. Ramos. As I watched, she lifted her head and listened. I could tell she heard it too. When she turned toward me, her eyes were wide.

I nodded my head to let her know I'd heard. Then I looked around the room.

None of the adults seemed to hear the sound. But Cali and I were paying more attention and watching for clues. I knew I noticed every new sound, every unusual movement.

The faint scratching noise got a little louder— something was right below our feet.

I walked over to help Cali hold her board steady. *Father in Heaven,* I thought, *what should we do now?*

"I don't like this," Cali said softly.

"Whatever it is, it's in the basement," I muttered. We tried to keep our voices low enough so Mr. Ramos couldn't hear.

Cali led me away from the group. "Or behind the door down there that Mr. Pike told us about. As soon as everyone leaves for lunch, I want to open that door and explore the mine. It's the only way we're going to find out what's going on," Cali said.

I wondered if she felt as brave as she sounded.

"I don't know if that's such a good idea," I said. My heart was beating so loud that I couldn't focus on the voices of anyone else in the room.

"You agreed to the idea last night," she pointed out.

"Yeah, I know, but right now I'm not so sure," I said.

"Why not?"

"Honestly, I'm scared."

"So am I, but I want to make sure this camp will be safe for kids. If it's not, we need to let someone else know," Cali argued.

"You're right. That doesn't make me any less scared, but . . ." I paused.

"But what?"

"We've got to do it," I finished.

Cali smiled. "Good. There's something real behind this whole Mad Miner myth. I believe the only way we can figure it out is by going into the mine. But we've got to be careful—real careful," she cautioned.

I nodded my head in agreement.

Cali looked around and noticed the adults had come to a stopping place in their tasks. "The others are starting to clear out to eat," she said. "Let me tell my mom that we'll be a little late for lunch."

Cali left the building with the rest of the work crew. Soon I stood there alone. The sounds in the basement got louder. A shiver shot up my spine, just like the chills I'd had when I first got to Camp Fearless.

Cali's returning footsteps on the old wooden floor made me jump.

"Are you ready?" she asked.

"Did you grab a flashlight?" I asked.

"Mr. Ramos left his on that old counter. I'm sure he won't mind if we borrow it. Let's go," she suggested.

We slowly walked toward the steps. I reached out and grabbed her by the arm to stop her at the top. "Before we go down there, I think we'd better pray."

"Yeah, that sounds like a good idea," she agreed.

We both bowed our heads, and I prayed. "Lord, please be with us as we try to solve the mystery of this mine. We want to know that Camp Fearless will be a safe place for campers to come in the future— a place to get to know you better. Lead us and keep us from harm as we search for clues. Amen."

I raised my head, took a deep breath, and began to descend the stairs. The sounds were faint but obviously coming from behind the wooden door to the mine. As we passed under the hole in the floorboards above, I looked up.

"Cali, shine the light up there," I requested in a whisper. I didn't want whatever was making the scraping noise to hear me. Together we examined the wood above us.

"Those cuts don't look fresh from down here either," I said, surprised.

Cali pointed down at our feet and quietly asked, "How long does sawdust usually hang around?"

I looked down and saw little curls of wood. "If those cuts were made a long time ago, this stuff would be gone. It's just like we thought. The boards were cut recently. The next question is, who did it?"

"There are some footprints in the dust over there," Cali whispered as she swept the flashlight along the floor. "They look like boot prints."

The footprints led to the heavy wooden door that

sealed the mine tunnel. We followed them and stood beside the door.

"Listen, that's where the sound is coming from," I quietly breathed out. I reached for the handle and noticed that the wooden plank used to lock the door was missing.

"This door isn't locked. Do you think the Madman of the Mine uses it to slip in and out of the camp at night?"

"Or is it open because someone wants us to go inside?" Cali questioned.

I gulped. Her question could be right on target. I thought about rescuing Mr. Thomas from the powder storage vault. Someone may have set a trap for us.

"Do you think we should go tell someone about this?" I asked.

Cali hesitated a moment, thinking. Then she said, "No. I don't want to give whatever is making those noises time to slip away. We've got to go in there now." She motioned for me to open the door.

The heavy door glided open silently. That surprised us both. Its ancient iron hinges should have been rusty and creaky. This door had been used recently and often.

Once inside we shut the big door behind us. I reached up and rubbed my finger along the hinge. I felt something slippery. I raised my finger to Cali's nose and she smelled it.

"That's oil," she whispered.

"Our legend takes pretty good care of his underground home," I said softly before starting down the mine tunnel. The noise grew louder and more distinct. We were headed in the right direction.

Cali kept the flashlight's beam on the ground. We couldn't see very far ahead of us. Abruptly the tunnel branched into two.

"Your choice," she said.

I nodded to the right. "I think the sounds are coming from that way."

"Wait a second," she whispered. "If you turn your head toward the left, it sounds like they could be coming from there instead. We must be hearing echoes."

"Then let's try the right first. If right is wrong, we'll just come back and try the left branch."

I started down the tunnel with Cali at my side. The farther we walked, the more narrow the tunnel became. Finally, we had to walk single file. Cali went ahead of me with the flashlight. After a few more steps, she gasped and grabbed at her face.

"Cali, what's wrong?" I asked in concern.

She turned back to me with a sheepish grin and said, "Spider webs."

I shivered, secretly glad she had gone first. About fifty feet later, the tunnel ended in an earthen wall.

"Hmm. I guess we have to go back and try the other way," I said.

Before Cali could voice her agreement, we heard a loud groaning. And it seemed close to us. Very close.

I felt panic course through me. "We're trapped," I whispered.

"I'm turning off the light," Cali said as she flipped the switch.

The darkness inside the tunnel was the thickest blackness I had ever experienced. Noises seemed to echo from every side of us. Then I realized they were echoes. Maybe nothing was headed toward us after all.

"Hold onto my shoulder. I'm going to lead us back out of here, and I don't want to lose you," I whispered. We started back down the tunnel, feeling our way along the hard, rocky wall.

"Our breathing sounds so loud," Cali whispered. "Every sound seems magnified in this darkness and silence."

"Silence?" I said, realizing she was right. "If someone were coming toward us, we'd be able to hear it. We're safe for now."

She turned the flashlight back on and we discovered that we had reached the branch in the tunnel. Left would take us back to the door and the general store. Ahead and to the right would lead us to where the noises must have been.

"Do you want to keep going or head back out for lunch?" I asked.

"We've already come this far. I really want to find out what's going on. Let's keep going."

The tunnel was deathly quiet now. Only our breathing and our quiet footsteps broke the silence. Were we really alone? Or was something waiting for us?

In a few minutes—which seemed like hours—we found ourselves in a little dug-out room. Another tunnel extended beyond it.

We stopped for a moment so Cali could examine the walls with her flashlight.

"This is really strange, Boone," she said.

"What is?"

"Some of these scratches look new. See here," she said, pointing excitedly. "Dust hasn't settled on this little ledge yet. And there's an awful lot of dust in the air here. This must be where the noise was coming from. I'm sure of it.

"This used to be a working silver mine. My guess is that someone's hoping to find a new deposit of silver," she finished.

"I guess we found what we were looking for. Now, let's get out of here."

"You got it, Boone," Cali answered. We walked quickly toward the tunnel that lead to the wooden door. In a few minutes we would be safe.

We were only a few feet from the door when I heard footsteps. I froze and put my finger to my mouth to warn Cali. Someone was on the other side of the door. The latch to open it clicked. Before we could run back down the tunnel, the door came swinging open.

Instinctivly, I flinched.

Then I recognized Mr. Ramos.

"So this is where you ran off to," he said when he regained his voice. I guess we had startled him too. "What are you two doing in here?" he asked.

"Just curious," I told him.

"We were looking for silver," Cali said.

"Did you find any?" he asked with a laugh.

We just smiled back.

"I got worried when you kids didn't show up for lunch. Something told me that you might do something foolish like going into one of the mine tunnels. It isn't safe. Do me a favor and never go in there again unless you're with an adult," he scolded.

"I'm sorry," Cali said. "You're right. It really wasn't a very smart thing for us to do. I guess our curiosity got the better of us."

"I'm sorry too," I added. Then I asked with a grin, "Is there any lunch left?"

"Sure, but you'd better hurry. The raccoon family may be dropping by again a little later," he said.

He led the way back up the stairs and toward the campfire. Then he excused himself to get something out of his truck.

As Cali and I filled our plates, I asked, "So, have you figured out what's going on here yet?"

"I've got some ideas. Help me put our clues together. There's a mythical Madman of the Mine, or at least Mr. Pike says there is. And we've had a number of experiences that seem designed to scare us away: Mr. Thomas got locked in a powder storage vault, we almost got creamed by a rock slide, we saw something in the Hanging Tree, something started a fire last night. Maybe the Madman of the Mine is real. Or maybe Mr. Pike is involved in some way," she concluded.

"How?" I asked.

"That I don't know. But I'm pretty sure he was the one in the tunnel with us today. He must've been looking for silver," she said.

As we looked for a place to sit and eat, I noticed Ezra Pike approaching with Mrs. Bittner. He was chewing on a piece of long grass as they talked.

"Hi, kids," Mrs. Bittner said. "Mr. Pike was just telling me more about the history of Fearless. This place sure has an interesting past."

"I'll bet," I said. I took a close look at the old caretaker's boots. I was startled. They showed no signs of having been in the dusty mine. Either he had cleaned them pretty well, or he hadn't been there at all.

"Listen, ma'am, it was right neighborly of y'all to feed me again. Maybe it won't be so bad havin' folks 'round this place. Long as you're a bit safer with yer campfires, that is," he smiled as he prepared to be on his way.

Everyone said good-bye, and Mr. Pike headed toward his cabin.

"Feed him? Did he have lunch with you?" Cali asked her mother.

"Yes, he did. He even helped me get the fire going first," Mrs. Bittner answered.

"Then he's been here since we went into the mine," I whispered to Cali. "That sure throws your solution to the mystery out the window. Mr. Pike couldn't have been the one in the tunnel."

Cali's face looked puzzled as she wrinkled her forehead. Then she said, "Not totally. It might just mean that he's not working alone."

"Then there might really be a Madman of the Mine?" I asked quietly.

Mrs. Bittner raised her voice to get everyone's attention. "Don't forget that every bit of food needs to get picked up and locked in the van after every meal."

"You've got it," Mr. Foster agreed. "Those raccoons woke me up twice last night. They managed to

113

get into several packages of good food and ruin them."

I thought about the shadows I had seen the night before. I wondered if they might have been made by one of the adults chasing raccoons. I sure hoped so.

When we finished eating, everyone pitched in to clean up the food area. Within minutes we were ready to get back to work. As the adults split up to finish their tasks, Mr. Ramos suggested that Cali and I take a hike.

"Why don't you check out the area above the camp?" he said. "See if there are any good trails for campers to use."

"Good idea," Cali agreed instantly.

"Remember though, no tunnels, and I do mean stay out of the mine. Just take in some clean, fresh air and sunshine," he said.

We promised. Eager to explore, we started up the steep slope to the north of the old mining town.

"There's where the rock slide was yesterday." Cali pointed to the area of disturbed rocks and earth.

"Let's climb up to where it started," I suggested.

"Sounds like a plan," Cali said as she led the way.

At the top of the slide, we looked for evidence of what had made the rocks begin to tumble. Even after searching the area carefully, neither of us found anything that looked out of the ordinary.

"Maybe an animal just kicked a loose rock," I decided, tired of looking. "Where to now?"

"Let's follow the trail we're on and head west."

I found it harder than I'd thought it would be to walk next to her along the rocky ridge.

After a few minutes Cali stopped and pointed over the valley. "Isn't it beautiful?" she asked. "This is a great place for a camp. I just hope we can solve the mystery and make this place safe." She paused and bit her lip, then spoke again, "Boone, do you think that Mr. Pike would try to scare us away because of the silver mine?"

"I guess anything's possible. The Bible even warns about the danger of loving money. But Mr. Pike was eating lunch with your parents when we heard someone in the mine. If he's involved, he must have a partner. But I haven't seen anyone else around Fearless."

"I wish I could make sense out of all these clues," she said.

"Me too," I said. "In the meantime, maybe walking will help us sort things out."

"I think I see another trail up there," she said. "Let's see where it goes."

"It's worth a try," I agreed. But I'd suddenly felt spooked by how alone we were. What I really wanted to do was plunge down the side of the mountain and keep going until I got home. Of course, that wasn't a good idea. Once I got started downhill, it would be impossible to stop. I'd end up in another rock slide. So I followed Cali up the hill.

Suddenly a small rock tumbled down the mountainside from above us.

I jumped, expecting another rock slide. "We'd better get out of here!" I yelled to Cali.

Before we could move, a deep voice bellowed, "Stop right where you are!"

I felt my legs turn to jelly.

We looked up. A man was walking toward us. He must have kicked the rock. He was carrying a rifle.

"What are you kids doing up here?" the man demanded.

"Hiking," I answered. I had a hard time keeping my voice steady.

"You missed the fork in the trail. It's back there right by the No Trespassing sign." The man pointed with the barrel of his rifle.

"Sir, we're really sorry. We were both so preoccupied with the view up here that we missed it. We wanted to see where this trail led," Cali explained.

"Where are your folks? You shouldn't be out here

all alone. It's not safe." Even though the man's voice was gruff, he didn't seem threatening anymore.

"My folks are down in Camp Fearless," Cali said quickly.

"Oh." The man nodded. "You part of that church group then?"

"Yes, sir," I answered.

"How's your camp project going?" the man asked. He pushed his hat back on his head a bit as he spoke.

"Fine," I answered. "There's a lot of work to do, but our church is filled with hard-working people."

"Hard work never hurt anyone," the man remarked. He looked past us toward Fearless.

"Sleep well last night?" he asked.

Cali and I exchanged a quick glance.

Without waiting for our reply, the man went on, "I've been here at Atlas Ski Resort for four years now. All I can say is I'd hate to spend a night in Fearless. It's one of the spookiest places I've ever seen once the sun goes down. If I were to give you church people some advice, I'd say get out of this place. Sell it and leave."

He looked at us carefully to see how his words affected us. I tried to keep my face expressionless.

"Did you kids happen to see anything?" he asked.

"Like what?" I asked.

"The Madman that haunts the mine or maybe ghostly figures in the Hanging Tree," he suggested.

"Why do you ask that?" I wanted to know.

"Just stories I heard. I'm glad I'm up here at the resort. Fearless is just too spooky for me," he said.

The man reached into his back pocket and pulled out a red bandanna. He opened it wide in the wind and rubbed the barrel of his rifle.

After warning us to keep off Atlas property, he turned and headed back down the trail. A few minutes later, we saw a trail of dust clouding up behind his Jeep.

"Wow, that was bizarre," I told Cali.

"I want to know why a ski resort's caretaker would need a rifle," Cali wondered aloud.

I shrugged. "Maybe he wants it for protection from wild animals. I'd like to know why he asked how we slept. Do you think he's really spooked by Fearless? Or was he referring to the fire we had?" I quizzed.

"If he was, I wonder if our favorite caretaker told him about the fire," Cali said.

"Maybe he's Mr. Pike's partner," I suggested.

"I don't think so; his clothes would have been dirtier from digging in the mine. But something tells me he might be a piece in this puzzle," Cali said.

We walked without speaking for about fifteen minutes. I looked down at the old mining camp below us. Then I broke the silence.

"You know, I just can't picture this place full of campers. If we keep getting spooked, won't every other kid that comes here feel the same way?" I asked.

"It's possible. I think we should talk to the adults. Maybe this isn't the best place for a church camp," Cali told me.

"I agree. We should tell—"

I abruptly stopped speaking.

"What's the matter?" Cali demanded.

"There!" I pointed to a huge boulder beside the trail ahead of us. "Someone just ducked out of sight. And boy, were his clothes a mess."

A small scatter of stones bounced away from the big rock.

My mouth suddenly went dry. We stood absolutely still.

Then, for a fraction of a second, I saw what looked like a tattered sleeve.

"Did you see that?" Cali's voice was tense.

"Yeah." My heart was pounding. "That's got to be the man I saw before."

Without stopping to think, Cali started along the trail toward the boulder. After a second, I followed at her heels. *Lord,* I thought, *this might be one of the dumbest things we'll ever do. Please send your guardian angels to protect us.*

"Cali, what are you doing?"

"I've got to see this guy up close so I can describe him to my folks."

"What if he comes after us?"

"Then we run like all get-out back toward the ski resort."

Seconds later she came to a halt.

"He's gone," she said softly.

"Probably ducked into an old tunnel." I was secretly relieved he had disappeared. I also hoped Cali would remember our promise to Mr. Ramos and not suggest we find and explore that tunnel.

"I guess that eliminates the man from the ski resort," she said pensively.

"What are you talking about?" I asked.

"He isn't linked to this because we just watched him drive off," she explained.

"I guess, but we still suspect Mr. Pike. And we know he couldn't have been in that tunnel with us because he was having lunch with your folks. Maybe it was the Madman of the Mine," I suggested.

Cali raised her eyebrows.

"Well, I'm not ruling anybody or anything out yet," I told her.

Cali nodded. She was quiet for a few minutes. I could tell she wanted to chase the man (or ghost) down.

Finally, she said, "Instead of trying to find out who was hiding behind that boulder, I guess we should head back to camp like the man from the ski resort told us to."

"Okay," I agreed quickly before she could change her mind. "We don't need to follow the trail. We can head down right here."

"Be careful, Boone. Don't go too fast. We've already seen how easily these rocks can start sliding," Cali warned.

"Right," I said as I led the way.

Before I knew it, however, my feet started slipping out from under me. The side of the mountain was steeper here than I thought it would be.

I shot my right foot toward a sturdy-looking rock. But it was loose too and started to tumble the second I put my weight on it.

"Boone!" Cali's cry of alarm echoed through the air.

I flailed my arms in an effort to catch my balance. But was impossible to slow my downhill slide. Both feet seemed to wave uselessly in the air.

As I bounced down the hill on my back, I heard Cali yell, "Boone! Look out. There's a drop just below you!"

By now I was sliding sideways down the steep slope. From the corner of my eye, I saw a rock ledge and then nothing but air beyond.

I cried out in terror. I realized that my own misstep was more dangerous than any mythical Mad Miner could be.

I frantically tried to slow my fall by pressing my hands against the ground. My right hand closed on something round and thin. My fingers tightened. I prayed that whatever I had grabbed would slow me down.

For an instant I thought my arm was going to be ripped off. But the tree root in my fist held fast. What I didn't know for sure was whether my grip was strong enough to save me.

Dust rose around me. With relief I saw I had stopped sliding. My arm ached, but I knew better than to relax my hold on the root.

When I felt for something to brace my feet against, I realized how close to disaster I had come. My feet dangled over the edge of the ledge.

"Hold on! I'm coming," called Cali.

Small rocks and more dirt fell toward me as Cali carefully picked her way down to help me.

"Here, take my hand," she said. "I've got my feet braced against a rock that seems solid."

Careful not to let go of the root, I turned until I could see Cali's outstretched hand. With trembling fingers I managed to get ahold of her hand. She helped me climb back up to solid ground.

"Are you all right?" Cali's voice was anxious. Her expression showed how frightened she was.

"I think so. Thanks." I rubbed at a skinned elbow, then began to brush off my clothing.

"Let's see if we can work our way away from this drop-off," Cali said finally.

"I'll follow you," I told her. "You're a better leader than I am."

She slowly led the way to safety.

When we reached level ground, I brushed more dirt off and rubbed at one knee. Then I laughed.

"What's so funny?"

"Me. The fact that my own carelessness almost got me killed. All this time I've been worrying about the Madman of the Mine. Maybe I should be paying more attention to what I'm doing."

Cali smiled at me. "Lead on."

Taking care not to slip, we made our way down the side of the mountain. When we reached Camp Fearless, we ran into Mrs. Williams.

"How are things going?" I asked.

"Couldn't be better, Boone," she said. "We have the shower up and working. The water's pretty cold, but at least we can get clean." Mrs. Williams was obviously pleased.

"Sounds good to me," I told her encouragingly.

Cali spotted Mr. Pike, the caretaker, standing in front of the old general store talking to several of our friends. She motioned for me to take a look.

"Hmm. I just had a thought. Could Mr. Pike have been disguised as the Mad Miner?" Cali asked. "Would he have had time to scare us then get here ahead of us?"

"It's possible, but remember he was outside when we heard the noises inside the mine," I reminded her.

"Wait a second. What if the guy from the resort made those noises?" she said rapidly.

I thought for a moment, then asked, "Do you think they're both after the silver?"

She nodded her head yes. "I haven't trusted Ezra Pike since he scared us in the store's basement. He's not very friendly. I think he's trying to scare us away. It must be because of the silver. Man, people do really stupid things for money."

"Let's find out how long he's been here," I suggested.

Cali walked over to the pump for a drink of cold water. I casually wandered next to Mr. Ramos.

"Has Mr. Pike been here long?" I asked quietly.

If Mr. Ramos was surprised that I whispered my question, he didn't show it.

"Ever since you two headed up the mountain."

"He didn't leave at all?" I asked, disappointed.

"Not that I can remember," Mr. Ramos answered

thoughtfully. "He was interested in how we planned to rig up the shower. He spent a long time watching that work crew."

Our suspicions about the caretaker were running us into dead-end after dead-end. Maybe the most natural explanation was something unnatural. Maybe there really was a ghostly Madman living in the darkness of the old mine tunnels.

My thoughts were abruptly interrupted by a blood-chilling scream.

We raced toward Cali. She stood sputtering by the water pump. Her face and hair were soaked.

"What happened?" I asked.

"I just wanted a drink of water. I pumped the lever and stuck my face under the spout. But the water came out faster than I expected. I got drenched," Cali shivered. "And this water is really cold!" She reached up to wring the water from her hair.

"I'm sorry if I scared everyone when I screamed," she added.

Mrs. Bittner brought her a towel to dry off.

"Well, now that the excitement's over, what do you say we get back to work?" Mr. Ramos said grinning.

I looked around for Mr. Pike, but he was gone. I figured he had walked back to his cabin.

When the others left us alone, I told Cali that the caretaker had been in Fearless when we saw the man on the mountainside.

"I was afraid that's what you'd tell me. Our clues

aren't coming together. I feel like we're missing something important," she said.

I agreed, but I wasn't ready to search for more clues quite yet. So we walked over to Mr. Ramos and I asked, "Mr. Ramos, what would you like us to do?"

"Well, I was about to put a second coat of paint on the church walls. I'd appreciate your help. You two can use the paint rollers, and I'll take the brush to do the trim work."

Together, the three of us walked through the town to the old church. Mr. Ramos popped open the paint cans and stirred their contents. "Using a paint roller isn't difficult," he explained. "It just takes a little care. Don't try to roll too fast. If you do, little drops of paint will fly off the roller. You'll spatter yourself and everything around you."

Mr. Ramos gave us each a roller and a roller pan filled with paint. As we worked, he said, "I don't think I told you two that Pastor Newman is coming up later today. He called me on my cell phone about half an hour ago."

"Why's he coming up?" Cali asked.

"Well, to be honest, I know that there are some odd things going on around here. So I called him early this morning for advice. Something tells me that you kids know more than I do about Camp Fearless."

I glanced at Cali and asked, "Like what, Mr. Ramos?"

"Something seems to have you two on edge. Care to talk about it?" he invited.

"Sure," I said. I was ready to confide in an adult about our fears.

Cali and I told him about the strange things we'd seen and heard. We suspected Mr. Pike was involved, but we couldn't prove it. We also talked about the mythical Madman of the Mine and running into the man from the ski resort. We pointed out that every time we thought we'd figured out the mystery, something else came up and sent us in another direction. Right now, our clues just didn't add up.

"I'm almost ready to believe in the ghost," Cali added.

"You kids have gathered a lot of good information. I think we need to share it with Pastor Newman when he gets here," Mr. Ramos said. He turned his head toward the open door. "That sounds like a car pulling up now. It may be him. I'll go see."

Before Mr. Ramos walked out of the building, he asked, "What do you think will happen next?"

"If someone's trying to scare us away, I expect he'll make a move while the pastor's here," I answered. "And since Cali and I have almost always been the target, I don't think we'll leave camp anytime soon." Cali and I concentrated on painting the walls. It felt good to have a task that could help us stay safe for a while. To help the job go more quickly, we sang all the camp songs we could think of.

Just as we finished the coat of paint, Mr. Thomas stuck his head in the door and called, "Time to call it a day and get cleaned up. Dinner will be ready soon. Oh, and Pastor Newman wants to talk to you before you hit the shower."

Cali and I crossed the future campgrounds to Pastor Newman. He was busy feeding wood to the fire, and he gave us a big smile when he looked up.

"I'm really glad to see some of the young people from our church up here helping. I want to express my thanks to you both," he said. "I'd also like to know a little more about what's been happening up here."

He settled himself on a log near the fire and invited us to do the same. Then he waved to Mr. Ramos to join us and continued, "It looks like I need your help."

"Sure," Cali said.

"What can we do, sir?" I asked.

Mr. Ramos settled himself on the log beside Pastor Newman.

"Mr. Ramos here told me an abbreviated version of what you told him, and I'm concerned. You see, if Camp Fearless is in any way dangerous for young campers, then the church may need to consider accepting the very generous offer we've had from someone who wants to buy it."

"Someone wants to buy Fearless?" Cali asked with surprise.

"Yes, the ski resort next door made an offer this

morning. Their timing seems almost too perfect. First I hear that Fearless may be dangerous, and then I get an unexpected offer to buy it," the pastor said.

I looked at Mr. Ramos. I was sure that he'd made the same connection I had.

As we discussed some of the strange happenings in Fearless, we made a few more connections between our clues.

Cali mentioned how Mr. Pike told us about the Hanging Tree. She and I had both seen something hanging from the tree. The funny thing was how abruptly Mr. Pike had started telling us about the tree—right after someone mentioned the ski lodge.

Mr. Ramos brought up the fire beside the church. Everyone had agreed that none of us could have started it. Then Mr. Pike had appeared and made a big deal out of telling us how dangerous fire could be to campers.

As I listened, I made another connection, and a simple plan began to form in my head.

Suddenly, I just knew it would work. With a triumphant grin, I shared my idea.

I had gathered up my towel and soap and rejoined my friends by the fire. I waited for the right moment, and it wasn't long before it came.

Ezra Pike sauntered up the pathway from his cabin. The old caretaker must have known that Pastor Newman had arrived. Mr. Pike strolled over to us.

"Howdy, sir," he greeted the pastor. "Somethin' tells me that yer the leader of these fine folk. The name's Pike, Ezra Pike. I'm the caretaker of this here place. Was wonderin' if'n you'd like me to continue doin' so fer the church."

"It's nice to meet you, Mr. Pike. I'm Reverend Newman, and that's a tempting offer you've made. But first I have some questions for you.

"The folks here have been telling me about some strange occurrences over the last two days. Maybe you could help me out by giving me a little background on the town of Fearless," the pastor said.

"The history here is pretty simple," Mr. Pike responded. "The mine is haunted. I 'spect the kids told you the story already. I don' think it's a safe place fer them. If yer askin' fer my advice, sir, I'd jist up and sell the town. I mean, if'n ya got a chance ta, that is."

"That's strange that you would bring up selling the land. I just got an offer from the Atlas Ski Resort. It was for a very generous amount," Pastor Newman said.

I interrupted the conversation to excuse myself, saying, "I'd like to stay and chat, but I've had a pretty grungy day. I think I'll go try out that ice cold shower of ours."

Pastor Newman told me to enjoy my shivers and we both laughed. It was then that Ezra Pike gave the sign that I was hoping for. He pulled his big red handkerchief from his back pocket, shook it in the air, and used it to wipe his brow. I had seen him snap the handkerchief in the air before, only this time I knew what it meant.

I walked off toward the shower while Mr. Ramos, Cali, Mr. Pike, and the pastor continued talking about the ski resort's offer.

Cali waited for a break in the conversation. Then she said, "Pastor Newman, I've been thinking a lot about Camp Fearless. Boone and I can't wait for the camp to open. Once it's cleaned and painted, it'll be great. Sure, some unusual things have happened here, but we've figured out some explanations for them."

"Golly, little lady. If'n there's a way ta explain ghosts away, then I want ta hear it myself," Mr. Pike said with a surprised laugh.

"Well, remember when my mom broke through the flooring in the old general store? Boone and I checked it out right after the accident. Someone had cut grooves into the boards to weaken them. They looked like fresh cuts. But later, when we went back to see them again, the grooves had been darkened to make them look old.

"Then I remembered Mr. Pike had told us that the Madman of the Mine had chased away the townspeople almost fifty years ago by weakening floorboards and tunnel supports. I realized someone had rubbed dirt or stain into the cuts to throw us off. I'll bet that someone didn't know we'd seen the fresh cuts."

Cali looked around the circle of faces to see how people were responding.

Then she continued, "A couple of times, Boone and I have seen someone sort of tattered and disfigured lurking at a distance, watching us. We almost began to believe in the Madman of the Mine. But maybe there's just a hiker out there who doesn't want to be social.

"And today we slipped into one of the mine tunnels

and discovered that someone was still digging around in the mine. There could be silver in there."

Mr. Ramos spoke. "But Mr. Markham told me that the town had died when the mine ran dry. I think you're letting your imagination get the better of you, Cali. Maybe it's time to stop thinking about ghost stories."

He stood with his back to Mr. Pike and flashed Cali a wink. Then he added, "Pastor, we've made some really great changes during our time here. Let's take a walk, and I'll show you some of them. In fact, why don't we all go? Mr. Pike, please feel free to join us. You might enjoy seeing the improvements we made this afternoon."

Without seeming to hurry, Mr. Ramos led everyone quickly toward the shower.

I stood in the shower, managing to avoid the flow of cold water. I waited and hoped. Hoped I was not wrong. Hoped Mr. Ramos had timed things exactly right.

Suddenly a hand in a tattered sleeve appeared over the top of the shower stall. I saw the hand and thought my heart might explode.

"Now!" I cried out loudly as I ducked farther into the corner. No way was that hand going to get ahold of me. What I hoped now was that Mr. Ramos had heard me.

"Surround the shower!" Mr. Ramos shouted.

"Someone on all sides. Move! Right this minute. Don't give him a chance to escape."

The next two minutes were total confusion. The adults surrounded the small shower. Cali dashed around to make sure every side was guarded.

"He's in here!" I yelled loudly. "Grab him!"

"Got him!" That was Mr. Thomas. Instantly the others rushed to his aid.

I dashed out of the shower to see who we'd caught. I was still dressed and had managed to stay fairly dry.

The disfigured-looking man struggled while seeming to protect his ankle, but the men holding him were strong. He couldn't escape.

I stared for a few seconds and realized the man was wearing a horrible mask. Then I turned to Pastor Newman.

"Pastor, if my hunch is right, the man inside that mask has a pretty strong reason to scare us away. And I think Ezra Pike has been helping him."

Several people turned to look for Mr. Pike.

"He's gone," Mrs. Bittner said, surprised. "The caretaker was here just a minute ago."

"Let's see what this man can tell us." Mr. Ramos said. He stepped forward and pulled off the mask of a disfigured face.

When he revealed who had worn the mask, Mrs. Bittner gasped. I swallowed hard. We all looked totally bewildered.

"It can't be!" Cali exclaimed.

We were staring at Mr. Pike. But how? The caretaker had been part of the crowd only moments before. How could he have slipped away to change so quickly into the costume?

The man standing before us drew back his lips in a snarl.

I realized something was wrong. Something was different. Then it came to me.

At the same instant Cali cried out, "He has all his front teeth. Mr. Pike is missing one."

"My guess is that we're looking at Ezra Pike's twin brother," I said with a grin. "They look just alike except this one hasn't lost one of his front teeth. And look at his swollen ankle. Cali, this is who we helped back to the cabin."

"This explains everything. This Mr. Pike played the part of the Mad Miner when the other Mr. Pike gave him a signal with his red handkerchief," Cali said immediately.

"What do you have to say for yourself, Mr. Pike?" Mr. Ramos stared directly into the man's eyes.

"Ain't much ta say. Ezra and I share the cabin. You folks just assumed he lived alone. The people from Atlas Ski Resort offered us a mighty nice deal if'n we could get you church folks ta give this place up. We reckoned if'n we got the kids scared 'nough, y'all would pack up an' leave. But those kids was too smart," Mr. Pike said.

"Why didn't Atlas try to buy the land before Mr. Markham gave it to the church?" Pastor Newman demanded.

The old man shrugged. "Maybe they didn't know it could be bought. None of us knew till we heard a buncha church-going folk was fixin' ta put a camp here."

"I guess I'll have to give the Atlas Ski Resort a call. This place is definitely not for sale now," Pastor Newman said. Everyone nodded their heads in agreement.

"You should ask him about the silver mine," I suggested.

"Ain't no silver. Wish there was, but there ain't nothin' here. Part of the caretakin' agreement was we could keep workin' the mine. I been adiggin' and hopin', but nothin' came from it," the twin answered.

"We should hold you for the sheriff. But if it's all right with the other members of the church here, I'd rather let you and your brother go, as long as you promise to leave the area."

After a few moments of thought, everyone agreed with Pastor Newman.

"But let me warn you," said the minister, "if you and your brother aren't out of Fearless by sundown tomorrow, I promise we'll press charges."

As the excitement died down, Cali and I walked slowly toward the church.

"I want to check out our paint job," I explained.

"Okay," Cali agreed. Then she added, "You know, Boone, I'm really glad that we'll be able to use this old mining town. It's too bad it's been neglected for so long. What a waste."

"Well, you know what I always say?" I asked.

"No, what?"

I flashed her a grin. "A mine is a terrible thing to waste."